Man in the Lake

Rhonda Pohs Mysteries Book One

Sherry Derr-Wille

Dedication

I would like to dedicate this book to my many fans who have been requesting murder mysteries for the past several years.

Chapter One

Jack Franks sat at his desk. His name plaque indicated he was the 'Chief of Police' and his uniform denoted his position. Unfortunately, his daily routine seemed about as exciting as watching grass grow on a hot summer afternoon.

He thought off all the episodes of *Law and Order* he'd watched over the years. Now those cops were doing real police work. They certainly weren't filling in for the crossing guard or helping Maude Paul get her cat out of the tree growing next to her porch.

It wasn't like he wanted to have an unsolved murder on his hands, but he did want to do more than act like Barney Fife on the old *Andy Griffith Show*. His officers were good at catching speeders in the speed trap out on the highway, but they did little else to earn their salaries.

Jack heard the phone ring, but ignored it. The office employed a secretary and that at least gave her something to do with her time every day.

It's probably another cat stuck in a tree. Certainly nothing to get excited about.

He went back to reading yesterday's weekly paper that just made it to his desk this morning. The news wasn't much different from what they published last week. Clara Johnson had her in-laws over for Sunday dinner so they could see the new baby and the Bradley twins celebrated their sixteenth birthday. Pete Brown's daughter got married and Harley Sacks' dog bit the mailman.

Rather than read anything further, he threw the paper on the desk and was set to go out for a walk when the phone on his desk rang.

"I think you ought to take this one, Chief," the secretary

said through the intercom.

Jack sighed deeply and picked up the receiver. "Franks here."

"Jack, this is Al. I just went out to Storrs Lake fishing and there's a man floating in the middle of the lake."

The panic in Al's voice was enough to send chilled shockwaves through Jack's body. "What do you mean there's a body floating in the lake?"

"Just what I said, asshole. I came out to fish and there's a body out in the middle of the lake. I haven't tried to go out and bring him in. He must have drowned. I've seen enough cop shows to know you don't touch things at a crime scene."

Jack rolled his eyes. He and Al had been friends since kindergarten and Al tended to exaggerate. If his friend were a woman, Jack's wife would have called him a 'drama queen'.

"Are you sure some kids didn't steal a mannequin from the mall and dump it into the lake?"

"Mannequin, hell, this ain't no mannequin. It's a man, and he's dead, I tell you. Now get your ass out here and investigate. That's your job, after all. You should do something to earn your pay other than just sitting in the office reading the paper."

Jack shoved the paper aside, ashamed everyone knew about his duties and reading the paper was about all he had to do on a Friday morning.

"Okay, I'll humor you, but if this is one of your practical jokes, so help me Hannah, you'll pay."

He hung up the phone, but it rang again before he had the chance to grab his keys and head out the door.

"This is another one for you to take," the secretary assured him.

"Franks here," he said, just as he always did when he answered the phone.

On the other end of the line, he could hear a woman crying. "This is Kitty Reedman. My husband, Karl, is missing."

Jack thought about Karl Reedman. He was hardly what anyone would call a 'faithful' husband. He recalled how Karl cheated on his first wife, Barbara, with his second wife, Marie. True to form, he cheated on Marie with his third wife, Christine. Just lately, he cheated on Christine with his current wife, Kitty, so why was Kitty so upset about him staying out all night? He was probably scouting out wife number five.

Envy was the word crossing Jack's mind when he thought about Karl's sexual exploits. The man had to have the stamina of a bull in a field full of cows in heat. The thought of a man being able to satisfy more than one woman at a time was mind-boggling. Hell, he had enough trouble with his wife of thirty years, to say nothing of having another on the side and probably out looking for the next sexual conquest.

"What do you mean he's missing, Kitty?"

"Oh, Jack, it's so terrible. Karl went out last night to get a pack of cigarettes and he never came back."

"Are you sure he's not with a friend?"

"Positive. I know what you're thinking. I know all about Susan Barclay. I called her and she hasn't seen him either. We have an open marriage. I know he has the sexual appetite of a much younger man, and one woman is never enough for him. That's why his first three marriages failed. He's not with his girlfriend and we're both worried. We've been calling everyone we could think of all morning, and no one has seen him."

"I'll investigate it, Kitty. I have something else to do first, then I'll be right over to file a missing person's report. I'll see you in a couple of hours."

He hung up the phone and wondered where in the hell he was going to find a missing person's report form. He knew they were somewhere in the office, but since his secretary, Melissa, arrived and reorganized the filing system, he couldn't find a damn thing.

"I need a missing person's report form," he said as he approached Melissa's desk. "Do you have any idea where I might find one?"

Melissa smiled in a way that said she knew exactly where to look. Damn, he hated the way she smiled when she knew where something was, and he didn't.

She got up from her desk chair and crossed to the file cabinets. Once there, she pulled open the one with the big black 'M' printed on the little card in the holder on the front.

He watched over her shoulder as she pulled out the file with the words 'Missing Persons' neatly printed on the top cut of the folder.

"Here you go, Chief. Is there any other paperwork you'll need this morning?"

"Thanks. I think this will do it."

He felt a bit sheepish as he left the office and went out to his car. It wouldn't take long for him to get out to the lake. The only thing he would be needing there was his digital camera in order to take a picture of the mannequin Al insisted was a dead body.

After turning down the road leading past the museum and the industrial park, he headed toward the unpaved portion of the road. When he went to high school, this was lovers' lane. He'd been down there parking with more than one girl when he was the big man on campus, a/k/a the 'captain of the football team'.

Al's beat-up pickup truck sat parked in the makeshift parking lot about fifty yards from the lake. It was here he got caught one night with his girlfriend necking in his '57 Chevy. If Al hadn't come into the parking area driving like a maniac, things might have gone further than kisses and heavy petting. Instead, Al buried his truck up to the axles and Jack ended up helping him dig the damn thing out. To say the moment was lost was an understatement, especially since the girl's father gave him hell for getting her home so late.

"Over here," Al called, as soon as Jack got out of the car.

Jack made his way across the almost knee-high grass, aware of how soggy the ground was from all the rain they'd had this spring.

"I'm coming, keep your pants on. It's so muddy out here, I could sink to my knees and be sucked into the mulch."

He looked past Al and saw the body of a naked man floating face down in the lake. "Holy shit, there's a naked man out there."

"That's what I've been trying to tell you. Do you think we ought to call for the rescue squad to come out here and get him back to shore?"

"How in the hell could someone get out there and drown?" Jack asked. "What did he do, take off his clothes and go out there to commit suicide? He could stand up and the water would be just over his waist. Have you touched anything out here?"

Al looked at him as though he'd lost his mind. "There's nothing to touch except the grass. I did notice some of the grass on the other side of the lake was beat down, but I didn't go over there to look."

Jack shifted his gaze from the tanned body and white ass of the man floating in the lake. The morning sun was doing its magic bringing the bent grass back to standing straight and tall.

Knowing the victim wasn't going anywhere, he left Al and headed around to the other side of the lake. Since the only access to that area was through the gravel pit, he knew he'd have to look there as well. Jack thanked his lucky stars there'd been no rain, as droplets of blood clung to the grass, indicating the path the body was dragged to get to the lake.

After taking several pictures, he turned on his cell and called the county sheriff's office. There was a fine line where this crime was concerned. Technically, the lake was within the city limits, but the gravel pit sat in the jurisdiction of the county. With the body being found in the city limits and the scene of the crime in the county, he knew the investigation would be a joint effort.

An hour later, several deputies, as well as the sheriff joined Jack.

"What made you decide this wasn't a simple drowning, Jack?" Sheriff Cantwell asked.

"It was Al Pardee who first saw the body. When he got out here, he said the grass on this side of the lake was bent. I decided it was best to come over here and investigate since the body wasn't going to get away from me."

The sheriff nodded. "Do you have a boat you can take out there and retrieve the body?"

"I can tell you aren't from town. The entire lake is only waist deep. You can't launch a boat in anything that shallow."

"Just how the hell do you expect to get the body to shore?"

Jack was getting more and more annoyed with the sheriff. The fact he said 'you' rather than 'we' irritated Jack.

"I can check and see if Al has waders in his truck. If he does, I'll go out there and pull the body to shore."

The sheriff looked at him as if he'd lost his mind.

"Do you have any better ideas on how we can reel him in?"

"I hadn't given it much thought. I figured we'd just go out there in a boat and get him. Guess it's a bit more complicated than I thought."

"Look Sheriff, I've been around this lake all my life. Now if it were the lake west of town, your idea of a boat would work. This one is different. If it weren't for all the rain we've had this spring, we'd be looking at a swamp rather than a lake. Calling it a 'lake' has always been a joke. Now if you'll excuse me, I'll go back around the lake and pull in my body."

"Your body? This is *our* jurisdiction."

"He may have been killed in your jurisdiction, but he was dumped in mine. The way I see it, if you scratch my back, I'll scratch yours."

"I'll go with you to make sure you don't muck up the evidence," Sheriff Cantwell proclaimed.

Jack laughed to himself. How in the hell could he muck up the evidence any more than it already was? The poor schmuck had been floating in the lake for God only knew how long. Any evidence would be completely waterlogged by now.

As they headed back around the lake Jack could hear Cantwell swearing about the mud and the muck. It was evident he didn't want to get his highly polished shoes all muddy.

Once back to where Al stood, Jack saw his friend was now grinning like a damned Cheshire cat.

"How do you plan to get him out of there?" Al questioned.

"I'm hoping you have your waders and boots in the truck. It looks like I'm going to go out there and drag him in."

Al laughed, like the idiot he was, and walked to his truck. The damn fool would probably hang around with that shit eating grin on his face until Jack pulled the body in.

By the time Jack pulled on the waders, at least a half dozen officers were standing on the shore, along with the coroner. From the looks on everyone's face, he knew they were grateful he was the one walking out through the murky water. Even though it was only late June, the water was already green. This had been a strange year with almost steady rain combined with an early heat wave.

Even though the waders and boots were a bit too large, it was better than walking out there unprotected. He felt his feet sink into the muddy lake bottom. Slogging through the mud made for slow going,

He finally got to the body and reached out to touch it. His initial reaction was to jerk away from the cold dead skin. With so many people watching his every move, he started back to shore with the dead weight in tow.

Once back at the shoreline, Sheriff Cantwell and two of his deputies helped get the victim out of the water. As soon as they turned the body over, Jack swallowed down the vomit threatening to erupt at any moment. Someone had shot the poor bastard in the nuts and cut off his pecker. To add insult to injury, he'd taken a shotgun blast to the face, obliterating his facial features.

"Holy shit, how in the hell are we going to identify this guy?" Cantwell asked.

"That will be my job," the coroner replied. "Between fingerprints and DNA, I might have an answer for you in a week or so."

"A week or so?" Cantwell echoed. "We need answers now."

The radio attached to the sheriff's shoulder crackled indicating a transmission would soon follow.

"We found something over here," the disembodied voice said.

"Don't beat around the bush. What did you find?"

"Well…ah…it's a guy's pecker."

Kitty Reedman's call resounded in Jack's mind. "Ask him if it's pierced," Jack said.

Cantwell looked at him skeptically, but repeated the request.

"It certainly is," came the reply. "Not only that, it's tattooed with a naked woman."

Jack nearly choked. He'd forgotten the tattoo Karl bragged about getting.

"I'm positive our victim is Karl Reedman. His wife called him in as a missing person right after I got the call about the floater."

Jack checked his watch. "I told her I'd be over there to file a report two hours ago."

"Are you sure?"

Jack wanted to laugh in the sheriff's face, but he remained professional. "Look Cantwell, this is a small town. From the looks of the guy, he's in his fifties, he's going bald, and your boys found his pecker over in the gravel pit, complete with piercing and tattoo. Considering Karl's the only person in town with the balls to have both procedures done then brag about them, it must be him. Besides, he's a missing person."

"Makes sense," the sheriff agreed.

Jack smiled at the slight victory he'd won over the sheriff in the turf war over this murder. Turning away, he took out his cell phone. Kitty would have to be notified and the best person he could think of to do it was the only female officer on his small police force.

When the city council first suggested hiring a woman, he fought them tooth and nail, but he'd been outnumbered. At least Rhonda was willing to go through grief training. She'd made herself an asset to the department when it came to telling families someone they loved wouldn't be coming home because of a car accident.

Chapter Two

Rhonda Pohs pulled her cruiser in front of the police station. She was happy when Officer Tews relieved her from speed trap duty. Everyone knew it was there and drove slowly until they were beyond radar range.

"Hi, Mel," she said as she entered the office. "Anything new?"

"The chief got a couple of calls this morning, but since then it's been quiet. I'm glad to see you though, since I need a bathroom break. I'll be right back. In this job, I've learned how to pee fast."

Rhonda laughed at Melissa's joke at her own expense before sitting down at the desk. No sooner did she get seated at the desk than the phone rang.

"Is this Melissa?" the woman on the end of the line asked.

"No, this is Officer Pohs. What can I do to help you?"

"Well, this is Kitty Reedman. I talked to that piece of crap Chief Franks three hours ago and reported my husband missing. He said he'd be here within a couple of hours to file a report. This is ridiculous. I'm a taxpayer. I pay his salary. He shouldn't keep me waiting like this."

"I'm sorry for the delay, Mrs. Reedman. I'll pick up the forms I need and be right over."

After verifying the address, Rhonda pulled the missing person's report form from the file.

"I hope it was quiet while I was gone," Melissa said, as she returned to her desk.

"Just a call from a very unhappy Kitty Reedman."

"Hasn't the chief been there yet?"

"It doesn't sound that way. I can't say I blame him. I've known Kitty all my life. We went to high school together. It doesn't surprise me to hear Karl is missing, I'd drop out of sight too if I had to put up with her twenty-four seven."

Rhonda and Melissa shared a laugh about the way Kitty Reedman reacted to Jack's snub before Rhonda went back out to her car. She'd just put the cruiser in reverse when her cell phone rang. Shoving the gearshift back into park, she answered it.

"Officer Pohs here."

"Where are you, Rhonda?"

She immediately recognized the chief's voice.

"I'm at the office getting ready to go over to pacify Kitty Reedman."

"If that's the case, I'm glad I reached you. I need to send you over there to tell Kitty someone murdered her husband."

The word *murdered* echoed through Rhonda's mind. There hadn't been a murder in this town in over twenty years. At the time, a friend of hers had been murdered by her brother. There hadn't been a trial because the doctors proclaimed the young man to be insane and sent him to the state mental hospital.

"Are you sure?"

"Positive. I identified the body. I'm on my way in, so if you can bring Kitty and Susan to the office, I'll talk to them both at the same time. Kitty told me Susan is at the house with her and they've been making calls all night trying to find him."

Rhonda agreed and proceeded to back out from the stall. She'd heard all about Reedman's affair with Susan. It wasn't much of a secret, especially since the rumor mill said they were doing a threesome on occasion. She'd often wondered about Kitty's sexuality in high school, but never said anything. The latest tidbit she heard was Kitty was bisexual.

When the Reedman mansion came into sight, Rhonda set aside her mental ramblings. After pulling up into the circular drive, she got out of the car and walked to the front door. Her finger hardly left the bell when the door opened.

To say Kitty looked like hell was a gross understatement, Mascara that was usually thickly applied, now ran down her cheeks in rivulets. These weren't the crocodile tears Rhonda remembered seeing from families in the past. Kitty was genuinely upset.

"Oh, Rhonda, it's you. I didn't recognize your married name. I'm going out of my mind with worry. How could it take this long to buy a package of cigarettes?"

Rhonda swallowed hard. She knew one of the reasons she'd been hired was to do death notifications. She'd taken several courses on the subject, but it never got easier.

"There's no easy way to say this, Kitty. Are you alone?"

More tears washed down Kitty's cheeks. "Suzie is here with me. Won't you come into the library? If it's bad news, we should be together."

Rhonda followed Kitty through the elegant foyer and down the hall to the library. Glass French doors guarded the entrance to the book-lined room.

Susan Barclay sat ono a floral loveseat that looked completely out of place in the room dominated by leather furniture. She looked as disheveled as Kitty.

"Before I came over here, I had a call from Chief Franks. He's found Mr. Reedman."

"Oh, dear," Kitty gasped, trying hard to remain in control. "Was he in an accident? What hospital is he in?"

Before saying anything further, Rhonda scanned the faces of the two women in the room with her. Both were white with dread.

"Chief Franks was called out to Storrs Lake this morning. That's why he didn't get here when he said he would. I'm sorry to have to tell you this, but Mr. Reedman has been murdered."

Kitty and Susan clung to each other for support.

"How?" Susan asked.

"All I know is that a body was found floating in the lake. Chief Franks identified it as Mr. Reedman."

"H-He could be wrong," Kitty stammered.

"I doubt it. He told me it was a positive identification. He asked me to bring both of you down to the station. He wants to meet with you in his office."

The two women stared at her in disbelief. It was the reaction she'd seen too many times in the past when she'd done death notifications for the department. "I have the cruiser out front. I can take you there. I doubt either of you are up to driving into town."

Obediently, the women followed her out to the car and seated themselves in the back seat.

~ * ~

Jack sat in his office, trying to compose his thoughts. The grizzly sight of Karl's mutilated body seemed to be burned into his memory. Although it was almost time for lunch, the thought of eating anything made his stomach churn.

"Mrs. Reedman and Ms. Barclay are here," Melissa's voice came over the intercom.

"Send them into my office and find Sheriff Cantwell. I'm sure he wants to be in on this interview as well."

It irritated him no end that Cantwell made a beeline for the break room and the donuts Melissa brought in fresh daily. The man had to be a cold-hearted son of a bitch if he could think of filling his face after what they'd seen at the lake this morning.

He had no time to dwell on Cantwell, as Rhonda escorted the wife as well as the mistress into his office.

"Is it true?" Kitty blurted out. "Is Karl dead?"

"Yes, Kitty, I'm afraid everything Rhonda told you is true. I told you I had something else to do this morning before

I came over to file the missing person's report. That something was to investigate a man floating in the lake. When I got there and retrieved the body, it was Karl."

"Who would do such a thing to Sweetums?" Kitty choked out between sobs.

Her choice of pet names was enough to make Jack gag.

"That's exactly what we're wondering, Mrs. Reedman," Sheriff Cantwell said, as he made a grand entrance into the office.

Jack noticed the trace of powdered sugar clinging to Cantwell's mustache.

"Have you been having any problems in your marriage?" Cantwell asked, as he nodded toward Susan.

"Oh, good heavens, no. We were supposed to have a threesome last night, but Suzie had something come up. We rescheduled it for tonight. When Sweetums didn't come home, I called Suzie, but she'd just gotten home and hadn't seen him."

The sheriff jotted notes furiously. "Just where were you last night, Ms. Barclay?"

Jack noted the smile crossing Susan's lips.

"I'm a sex therapist and I had an emergency session with a couple in crisis."

"What is the name of these clients?" Cantwell questioned, skeptically.

"You know I can't divulge their names, but I do have a business card. My secretary can give you the schedule for last night."

Jack almost choked over Susan calling herself a sex therapist. He always thought she was a high-paid call girl, but how many call girls had secretaries?

"That brings me to you, Mrs. Reedman. Where were you last night?"

"You can call our cook, Samantha. When Karl went out, we decided to play a game of cribbage. We played until well after ten. That's when I started calling Karl's cell phone. I figured he's met up with one of his associates and got to talking. I know how it is when he's enjoying a conversation. He seems to lose all track of time. I never imagined he was being killed."

Jack doubted Kitty's story. As far as he was concerned, he didn't think she had the brains to know which cards added up to fifteen, much less to grasp the concept of the game.

"You can't possibly think we had anything to do with this, do you?" Susan asked once Sheriff Cantwell left the room to check on their alibis.

"At this point in the investigation, everyone is a suspect," Jack advised her in his best imitation of Lenny Brisco's voice from 'Law and Order'. "Of course, the most logical place to start is with those closest to the victim."

"It makes sense, Suzie," Kitty said between sobs.

"I suppose it does, but I don't like being treated like a suspect," Susan whined.

Jack shook his head in disbelief. Didn't these women watch television? If they did, they'd realize those closest to the victim were always the first ones the police suspected.

"I have good news for you ladies," Sheriff Cantwell said, when he returned to the room. "Your alibis checked out. You're both free to go."

"Can we see Karl's body?" Kitty asked.

Jack inwardly groaned. How could he begin to explain the damage done to Karl's body without grossing the women out completely.

"The body was badly mutilated," Sheriff Cantwell replied. "I think it's best if you remember him the way he looked the last time you saw him."

"Mutilated?" Kitty questioned. "If that's so, how could you have identified him? How do you even know it's Karl?"

"Ah…well," Jack stammered. "He does have a very distinctive penis."

"You undressed him?" Susan asked.

"No, whoever killed him did that. We found him floating naked in Storrs Lake."

Both women gasped and began to cry all over again. Damn he hated crying women.

"What about his clothes?" Kitty inquired.

"We haven't found them yet."

"He had several hundred dollars in his wallet, you have to find it."

Jack recalled Karl always carried large amounts of cash. If the murder hadn't been so brutal and personal, they'd be looking for a robber. Instead, it was someone who wanted to humiliate Karl, while making it look like a mugging gone badly. Why else would they make him strip naked before they killed him?

"Whatever we find will be evidence," Sheriff Cantwell advised them. "When and if we find his clothing or anything else he might have had on him, we'll let you know."

Jack knew the answer they received from Cantwell wasn't what they wanted to hear, but it was the truth. The fact that Karl's clothing hadn't been found only added to the mystery. Why take a man's clothing when the murderer could have emptied the wallet and fled the scene?

"Like Sheriff Cantwell said, you ladies are free to go. Since Rhonda brought you ladies here, I suggest she take you home."

~ * ~

Rhonda waited outside the chief's office. Through the closed door, she could hear little of the conversation between the two men and the women she brought into the station.

When Jack opened the door, he motioned her to come into his office. "The ladies are free to go," he said.

As soon as she entered the office, she saw Kitty and

Susan sitting in the two chairs across the desk from the chief's big leather chair, clinging to each other, their bodies wracked with sobs.

"I can take you home," she offered as she approached them.

"Don't we have to go to the funeral home, or something."

"Not just yet. Mr. Reedman is at the coroner's office. They'll have to do an autopsy. I'm sure he won't be released to the funeral home until Monday at the earliest. Things don't move very fast over the weekend."

Kitty nodded. Together, they went out to the car. As they drove through town toward the Reedman mansion. Rhonda wondered how long it would take for the gossip grapevine to be buzzing with the news Karl Reedman had been murdered out at the lake.

At the office she'd been told that Al Pardee was the one who found the body. Considering he was the biggest blabbermouth in town, it wouldn't be long before everyone was locking and double locking their doors in fear of a murderer on the loose.

Chapter Three

By Monday morning, the rumors at the coffee shop were running rampant. Jack knew the preliminary autopsy report wouldn't arrive until at least the afternoon, meaning the investigation went absolutely nowhere over the weekend.

"So, what do you make of this murder, Chief?" Andy Parker, the local barber asked. "I heard they cut off Karl's pecker. Is that true?"

Jack damned Al and his big mouth. Of course, the scene he'd observed out at the lake was too juicy a bit of gossip not to pass it on. What was the most disturbing was that the people of this town had already heard all the gruesome details. "That's right."

"I'll bet it was some woman who figured she wanted more than a one-night stand and Karl wasn't willing to give it to her. Why would he want to take a little one-night stand over two hotties like Kitty and Susan?"

"Hell, no," Mike Jacobs, a coffee shop regular commented. "My money is on a husband to the floozie. I know I was plenty mad when Karl made a pass at my wife. Thank goodness she had the good sense to laugh in his face."

Jack took mental note to question Mike further if necessary. "Any idea who Karl has been putting the moves on lately?"

"Let's see," Mike replied. "I've heard he propositioned Eileen McChesney and Irene Colby. The word is he's been with Phyllis Abernathy, Caroline Adams and of course, Susan Barclay. Other than that, I'm not too sure, but the list has to be massive. He used to brag about how much the women liked that pierced and tattooed dick of his."

Mike's comment started a conversation with the names of almost every married man in town mentioned, causing Jack to make furious notes concerning what he heard.

Once back at the office, he found the autopsy report sitting in the center of his desktop. He picked up the report and debated about opening it. If the shot to his nuts didn't kill Karl, the one to his face surely did, to say nothing of the slicing off his pecker. It certainly didn't matter which one killed him, he was dead, and it was up to Jack along with Sheriff Cantwell to find out who did the dirty deed.

He pulled out his notes and read the list of names he'd heard at the coffee shop. On his own, he could add at least ten to fifteen more. Karl had been a busy boy over the years, and he'd pissed off a lot of husbands.

Most of the names he had could and would undoubtedly turn out to be dead ends. This was a crime of passion and probably done by one of the husbands of Karl's latest conquests. Some men, especially the young ones, didn't want an old guy putting the moves on their girlfriends, fiancés, or wives.

"Sheriff Cantwell is on the line for you," Melissa said over the intercom.

Jack took a deep breath to compose himself. The last thing he wanted was to have to talk to the sheriff, but it couldn't be avoided. Before picking up the phone he flipped open the autopsy report.

"Franks here," he finally answered.

"It took you long enough," Cantwell accused. "Were you on a donut break?"

Like he has anything to talk about. He certainly ate his share when he was here on Friday.

"I was in the middle of reading the autopsy report," Jack lied.

"What do you make of it? The poor bastard must have suffered. I can't imagine being alive and having my Johnson whacked off."

Jack cringed. He hadn't read any of the report. If the truth were known, he didn't want to read it. The information he knew it would contain made him sick to his stomach.

"The way I see it, this was a crime of passion. That said, I think we're going to need extra help up here. Karl propositioned almost every woman in town. That makes every one of their husbands a suspect."

"Even you?"

The question came as an irritation. "I admit, I was pissed as hell when he came on to my wife, but that was ten years ago. At the time, she told him to get lost. Karl was such an old horn dog, he probably hit on one of the young girls in town and her boyfriend went ballistic."

Cantwell agreed and prolonged the conversation even further by making other suggestions Jack wanted no part of.

A knock at the door, almost as soon as he hung up the phone, irritated him further.

"Enter," he called.

Rhonda came into his office. He wondered why she wasn't out on the highway running the speed trap.

"I just got off the phone with Kitty, Chief. She says they released the body this morning and she's planning the funeral for Wednesday morning."

"So?" Jack replied. "What does that have to do with us?"

She gave him one of those looks that he completely exasperated her. He knew it came from all those damn courses the kids today took. When he started with the city, he was fresh out of high school and learned what he needed to know by the seat of his pants.

"Since this is an ongoing murder investigation, I thought you might want to assign an officer to go the visitation and the funeral to see who shows up."

Jack nodded. He should have thought of that, but there

was just too much going on to remember everything.

"That sounds like an ideal assignment for you, Rhonda, considering you went to high school with Kitty. If you go out of uniform, you should blend right in. Just out of curiosity, why are you in the office and not out on the highway?"

"I don't come up in the rotation until Wednesday. It's a good thing, too, since Kitty has been calling me steadily since Friday."

"Calling you? Why hasn't she been calling me?"

"It's a woman thing. Since we went to school together, she feels she can trust me more than she does you or Sheriff Cantwell.

At first, the fact Kitty called Rhonda and not him annoyed Jack no end, it just wasn't right to think Rhonda could so easily appeal to flies with honey than with vinegar. Women were more likely to confide in their own kind than the opposite sex.

"As a matter of fact, I think you should be assigned to the grieving widow along with the mistress, at least until the funeral is over."

~ * ~

Rhonda let out a long sigh of relief as she left the chief's office. All weekend, she'd been spending most of her free time at the Reedman mansion.

In school, she and Kitty ran in entirely different circles. Kitty was the head cheerleader, homecoming queen and prom queen, while Rhonda worked her butt off to maintain her three point seven-four grade point average.

The fifteen years since graduation leveled the playing field between them. Now she was acting more like a friend than one of the snobby girls who looked down their noses on the nerds who were more interested in good grades than the latest fashion.

Kitty answered the door wearing a pair of cut-off shorts, a loose-fitting top, and flip-flops. Her face had been scrubbed clean of makeup and her eyes showed her lack of sleep.

"Oh, Rhonda, I'm so glad to see you. I know it's part of your job, but I'm afraid to be here alone."

Rhonda looked at Kitty skeptically. "What do you mean you're frightened? You're hardly alone here. There's you cook and groundskeeper, to say nothing of Susan."

"Susan has clients scheduled and is grieving privately. Our cook has been with Karl for over twenty years, She's so distraught over his death, I sent her to visit her son in Monroe. Since the groundskeeper is her husband, he went with her. At the time it seemed logical. Now I'm not so sure. I've been getting a lot of phone calls."

"What kind of phone calls?" Rhonda questioned.

"On Saturday and Sunday, they were condolence calls from Karl's friend, but this morning they turned threatening. I stopped answering them and let the machine pick up."

"Would you mind if I listened to them?"

"Only if I don't have to listen. The ones I picked up were so terrible, I couldn't stand to listen anymore. The machine is in the library. While you listen, I'll go out to the kitchen and make us some iced tea."

Once Kitty left, Rhonda checked the answering machine. It registered twenty-seven calls where messages were left and a total of thirty-five new calls.

Before she could press play, the phone rang. Rather than answer, she listened to see if the caller would leave a message.

"What's the matter, bitch? Are you too scared to talk to me? It doesn't matter. Your bastard of a husband got exactly what he deserved. It's too bad someone didn't off him years ago and save the women of this town from him."

She checked the remainder of the calls. To her dismay, the caller or callers blocked their numbers from showing up on the caller ID. All twenty-eight of the threatening calls seemed to have come from three different people, but she didn't recognize any of their voices.

"Did you hear them?" Kitty asked, as she entered the room, carrying a tray with a pitcher of iced tea and two tall ice filled glasses.

"I just finished listening to them. It seems as though there are three different callers, but they've managed to block their numbers from the caller ID. You were right not to answer any of them. That way you have a record of what they've been saying."

"What happens when the machine runs out of tape?"

Rhonda smiled. She'd noticed the machine was an older model. "Have you checked your husband's desk? It's possible he has a backup tape. If not, we'll make a trip to the office supply store. My husband has a tape machine and I know they carry the replacement tapes. We'll be able to get several of them."

"Maybe I should just set up the new system Karl got for his birthday last week. He was going to install it over the weekend.

"That would be perfect. If you have it handy, I can install it for you."

She was pleased to see there was a digital voice mailbox within the phone, so messages could be heard when they were first made, digitally recorded, and kept through a back-up system with the phone company.

After setting everything up, she listened as Kitty recorded the message. With everything up and running, Rhonda unplugged the old machine to take it to the station. Hopefully, someone from the county's IT department would be able to see who was making the calls.

Chapter Four

Jack no more than pulled into the parking lot of his office when several county deputies arrived.

"The sheriff told us you have a list of potential suspects," said the man who identified himself as Deputy Krueger.

"I don't know if you'd call them suspects. The victim was a ladies' man, I doubt you'll find a man in this town, even his so-called friends, who is sorry he's dead. He was a bit like a piranha fish. You know, they're beautiful to look at, but best to keep your distance because they're very dangerous.

"That's hard to believe," Deputy Krueger commented. "I've heard about how wealthy he was and how many donations he made to worthy causes. Isn't the new addition to the high school named after him?"

"Sure, it is. Wouldn't you expect to have an addition named after you if you donated three million dollars? Money never meant anything to him. He was born into it and made additional money daily from his investments. It's not like he ever had to work a day in his life. It gave him a lot of free time to carry out his other pursuits. Combine his fortune, slick line, and pierced dick to convince women to have a fling with him."

"So, the guy had a little extramarital fling, who doesn't?" the second deputy observed.

Jack groaned. It was evident this guy was thinking with the wrong head. If he voiced that opinion too loudly while interviewing the men on the list, there might be open hostilities.

~ * ~

Three hours later, Jack and the deputies finally finished compiling the list of names of people they wanted to question. With Rhonda babysitting and one officer working the speed trap, he'd have to pull at least two officers off patrol duty to bring in the men they wanted to question.

After calling in the two officers he wanted, Jack stepped out to the parking lot to have a cigarette. He hadn't gotten it lit before his cell phone rang.

"Chief, this is Rhonda."

Jack shook his head. He knew exactly who was calling. Her name came up on his caller ID. "Are you at the Reedman Mansion?"

"You know I am. That's what I'm calling you about. Kitty has been getting some terrible phone calls."

Jack rolled his eyes. He knew all about what women thought were terrible. They were probably little more than a broken fingernail. His wife always made a mountain out of a molehill when she wanted his attention.

"What do you mean terrible?"

"Nasty, I'd call them threatening. The worst part is the cook and groundskeeper have gone to Monroe to stay with family for a few days to get away from all the publicity."

"Look, Rhonda, you're right there with her. What harm can come to her? You know what they say about sticks and stones. Would that husband of yours be upset if you camped out there for a couple of nights?"

"I've already talked to him about it. He's coming over to stay here as well."

Jack finished his conversation and hit the end button. With Rhonda's husband staying at the mansion, he would write these two women and their imaginary problems off his books.

~ * ~

Rhonda was seething when she got off the phone. She hated Chief Franks' condescending attitude when he talked to her. He certainly treated her like an inferior person. It seemed as though he was patting her on the head saying, 'run along like a good little girl'.

"Is he going to investigate the calls?" Kitty asked.

"He said he would," Rhonda lied.

She hated lying but she had no choice in the matter. Chief Franks didn't want to listen to anything Rhonda had to say. If any information was to be obtained, she knew it would be up to her to get it.

"I talked to my husband and he agreed to come here and stay with us, if it's all right with you."

The look on Kitty's face was one of pure relief. "Of course, I don't mind. It will be good to have guests for a while. I honestly don't like being in this big house all by myself and the phone calls don't make things any better. For a while, at least, I can pretend none of this ever happened. Can you believe the funeral director told me whoever murdered Karl cut off his penis? How could anyone do such a thing?"

Rhonda ached for Kitty. She'd asked the same questions when she first heard of the mutilation. It made no sense whatsoever.

By four, Rhonda's husband, Mark, arrived, suitcase in hand.

"Are you sure about this?" he asked when she met him at the door. "I'm no cop."

"Well, I am and the way you're built you can be our bodyguard. It's not like I'm expecting anything to happen, but you never know. The phone calls are scary to say the least."

"Oh, Mark," Kitty exclaimed when they entered the library. "I feel so much better knowing you're here."

Rhonda let Kitty gush over Mark. It was a normal reaction. Over the years, she'd become accustomed to women making a fuss over her six-foot, seven-inch, extremely handsome husband. In high school and college, he'd played varsity football and after graduation, he'd been drafted by the Green Bay Packers. He'd been cut early on, but the experience was worth it. Now he was coaching for the local high school and enjoying every minute of it.

"What would you girls like for dinner?" Mark asked, bringing Rhonda back into the conversation.

"Contrary to popular belief," Kitty began before Rhonda could reply. "I'm a decent cook. Karl always said he liked what his cook prepared for him, and he didn't marry me for my skills in the kitchen. I must admit, that hurt a bit, since I do enjoy cooking. I have gazpacho made and steaks ready for the grill. I do hope you can do the grilling, Mark. I was never comfortable cooking outside."

Rhonda wanted to laugh at the look of terror on Mark's face at the thought of cold soup. He was a meat and potatoes man, period. Even getting him to eat veggies was a hard task.

"Gaz what?" he questioned, once Kitty got up to go out to the kitchen.

"It's a cold soup. I think you'll like it."

Rhonda gave him a look she prayed said he'd eat it and like it.

Kitty brought out large bowls of the cold soup and even Rhonda wondered about eating it but said nothing.

"Well," he replied, winking broadly at Rhonda. "I'm always open to new things and about the grill, you're talking to the master chef in that department."

Rhonda could tell Mark was laying it on thick, but that was alright, especially since Kitty Reedman wasn't his type.

Before dinner, Kitty insisted they have cocktails. Considering Rhonda was officially off duty, she accepted a glass of wine, while Mark had a beer and Kitty a vodka martini.

"So," Rhonda began, once they were seated on the

patio. "What is the relationship between you and Susan?"

Kitty sipped her martini before answering. "I've been seeing Susan professionally for years. Although I adore sex with men, I also like it with women. After we got married, I knew Karl wanted more than one partner, so I introduced him to Susan. It gave me the best of two worlds."

"How did your husband feel about that?" Mark inquired.

"At first, he was a bit shy about it, but when he found out how much fun a threesome could be, he changed his mind. We each still had our time alone with him, but our time together was equally fulfilling, especially for me."

Rhonda harbored doubts about such a relationship, but the stories she'd heard about Karl Reedman since the murder seemed to substantiate everything Kitty just told them.

Mark cast Rhonda a glance that said he wanted nothing to do with anything so kinky.

Rhonda could feel the wine going to her head. It was rare that she drank anything stronger than soda, even while she was off on the weekends. Tonight, the chilled Lambrusco tasted good.

Before Mark took over his duties at the grill, Kitty served them the cold soup. Rhonda had heard about it before, but never tasted it. To her surprise, it was quite good. Even Mark said he'd enjoy having it again. Once this was over, she'd have to search the Internet for a recipe.

"Is there anyone else you can think of who might want your husband dead?" Rhonda asked while Mark put on the steaks.

Fresh tears welled up in Kitty's eyes. "I wish I knew. Before we were married, he had a discussion with his son and daughter about our relationship. They wanted to know what our marriage would mean for their inheritance. His son was from his first wife and his daughter from his second, so by the time I came along they were used to stepmothers coming and going with great regularity. We talked about their inheritance and Karl assured them their money was secure and wouldn't go to me."

"What will you get as an inheritance?" Rhonda pressed.

"The same as all his other wives. Karl invested five hundred thousand dollars in our names. It was done as a wedding gift. I even signed a paper about it when we got married, saying I wouldn't contest the will and ask for more of his money."

"So, what do you do now?" Mark inquired.

"I'll stay here at the house until the estate is settled and I get a full-time job. Thank goodness, I kept in touch with my boss from before I got married. He said I could come back anytime."

"Where were you working?" Rhonda asked.

Since she and Kitty hadn't been close, she hadn't kept tabs on her whereabouts.

"It's a computer information business in Madison called 'The Computer Guru'. I've been doing some consulting work for them ever since I got married. He called on Sunday after he heard about Karl's murder and told me I could come back whenever I was ready. He even suggested I come to Madison and stay with him and his wife. I told him I thought my place was here."

"What will happen to this house?" This time it was Mark who asked the question.

"The will leaves it to his kids; with the stipulation the cook and groundskeeper will be able to stay on for the remainder of their lives. When we talked to them before we got married, they were quite disappointed about not being able to sell it. Donna posed the idea of making it into a bed and breakfast. Karl told her the decision would be between her and her brother, Brad. The last I heard, he thought it was a great idea as long as he didn't have to run it and she gave him part of the profits as co-owner."

Rhonda filed the information away in her mind. She wondered if the chief considered questioning Karl's kids. If Donna and her husband were anxious to start the business, it would be to her advantage to have her father dead and Kitty out of the house. If that were the case, the murder would be enough but wouldn't justify the mutilation of Karl's body, but it did give her motive.

Mark got up to check on the steaks and Kitty went to the kitchen to get the potatoes and vegetables, leaving Rhonda alone at the table on the patio. She was deep in thought when the ringing of the phone startled her. In order to monitor the message being left, she went into the library.

Kitty's prerecorded message just finished playing when Rhonda reached the table with the phone and answering machine on it.

I know you're avoiding me, bitch. Of course, that's what gold diggers like you do. You have no right to old man Reedman's money. His death was only the beginning. As his whore, you don't deserve to live. Be forewarned, you're next.

Cold chills ran down Rhonda's back. This call was different from the others Kitty received, even though the voice was familiar. This was a definite death threat. Her stomach churned as she turned and saw Kitty standing in the doorway.

"He means to kill me," Kitty gasped. "Oh, god, I don't want to die, not like Karl did."

"We won't let anything happen to you," Rhonda assured Kitty after taking her into a comforting embrace. "The steaks should be ready by now. We'll eat and decide what to do."

Although the table on the patio had been set, Rhonda insisted they move inside to the formal dining room.

"We're not staying here tonight," Mark insisted.

"You know we have to protect Kitty."

"We will, but not here. I think it's best if we make it look as if we're leaving Kitty alone. I'm sure if anyone is watching they'll be checking out the front of the house. Kitty, you'll change clothes with Rhonda and drive away in the cruiser. Rhonda, you'll take Kitty's overnight bag and cut through the woods. I'll pick you up on Townline Road. Since you'll be out of the house as soon as we are, you'll be out of danger and Kitty will be safe. We'll formulate a plan on how to proceed once we meet up."

Rhonda silently applauded Mark for the idea that should have been hers. She was just too damn close to this to be thinking rationally.

"Where will I go?" Kitty asked.

"You'll drive to the police station. Mark will follow you in the truck then veer off to pick me up. After that we'll pick you up there.

"I'll give the chief a heads-up on what we're doing. Just leave the keys in the cruiser. Whatever you do, don't go into the station."

Despite the severity of the situation, Kitty acted as though this was all a great game. It didn't take long for her to pack a suitcase and change clothes with Rhonda. Luckily, they were about the same size with the same hair color.

Rhonda watched as Mark and Kitty pulled out of the driveway. She was just about ready to set the auto timer for the lights and sneak out the back door when the phone rang. She listened intently to the message the caller left. This time it was the voice she referred to as caller number one.

I see that police woman and the other guy leave. With them gone, you're all alone. Be ready for us to come and visit, it's time for us to get what is ours.

Panic filled Rhonda. Before leaving the house, she activated her cell phone to call the chief. To her dismay, his voice mail picked up. Not wanting many more people to know their plans, she hesitated in calling 911.

Quickly, she grabbed both the overnight bag Mark brought for the two of them along with the one Kitty packed and took the steps to the exposed basement of the house. Stepping outside, she was relieved to see the sun setting. The shadows of evening were already beginning to cover the backyard, hiding her escape into the woods.

She'd just slipped into the cool darkness provided by the stand of trees when she heard a shot being fired at the front of the house Being securely hidden, but not far enough away to be out of earshot, she listened as a second round fired along with the sound of breaking glass. Going deeper into the woods, she again pulled out her cell phone and called dispatch, "Shots fired at the Reedman mansion," she whispered into the phone. "This is Officer Pohs."

"Where are you, officer?"

"That's not important. All you need to know is someone is trying to kill Kitty Reedman."

Her mind spun. At this point, she didn't want too many people to know Kitty was safe to say nothing about being alive and well.

Behind her, she heard an explosion. Turning around she saw the evening sky light up as part of the house erupted in flames. Hitting redial on her phone, she requested the fire department be sent to the address.

By the time she reached the road where she said she would meet Mark, her breath came in ragged gasps. In the distance she saw headlights, but waited until she recognized Mark's SUV before stepping out from the cover of the woods.

"What in the hell is going on?" Mark asked. "Why weren't you waiting along the side of the road?"

Rhonda nodded toward the smoke rising from the house they had just left. "Someone is trying to kill Kitty. As soon as the two of you left, they made a very threatening phone call. For now, it's best if she disappears. Thank God, I put the old answering machine in the cruiser. I don't know what part of the house they set on fire, but I'm afraid we might have lost the new machine. Before I heard the explosion, there were shots fired and I heard breaking glass."

"I've been giving this a lot of thought," Mark said. "I think we should take her up to my folks' cottage at the lake. No one will think to look for her there."

"No one will think to look for her anywhere. When I called dispatch, I told them she was in danger. Hopefully, we can make everyone think she was killed. I do like your idea of taking her up to the cottage. It's not unusual for us to go up there in the summer. With your parents on a three-week vacation in Africa, the cottage will be unused until they return, Hopefully, by the time they get home, this case will be solved, and the danger will be past."

Chapter Five

Jack's cell phone rang again. Before answering, he checked the caller ID. Just minutes earlier, Rhonda called, but he ignored it. He certainly didn't want to hear about crank calls and a silly woman's fears. When he saw the number for dispatch he answered immediately.

"Thought you'd want to know, Chief, there were shots fired at the Reedman mansion, Officer Pohs called it in, then called back and requested the fire department to be sent out there."

"I'm on my way," Jack replied. "Have you called the sheriff's office?"

"Cathy is on the line with them right now. I'm surprised Officer Pohs didn't call you directly."

"She might have, but I didn't hear it ring. I'll check my messages."

Sheepishly, he listened to the message Rhonda left earlier. Even if he took her call, he might not have thought it urgent. Considering the call from dispatch, he called Rhonda back.

"What's going on out there?" he asked, as soon as she answered.

He listened as she described the last two calls Kitty received, as well as the shots fired at the house and the fire.

"We're taking Kitty somewhere safe, but maybe you should run it past the county boys. I think it's best if everyone thinks she's dead."

Jack nodded his agreement with Rhonda's suggestion before verbally agreeing to it. "I'm making an executive decision here. The knowledge of Kitty being alive is something that is best left between the two of us. I'll handle the country boys. What about you, are you safe?"

"I'm fine. I was out of the house before the shots were fired. With Mark off for the summer, it's best if he stays with Kitty during the day. I'm planning to come into work as usual. I'll be here for my shift tomorrow."

Jack no more than ended the call when his phone rang again. This time it was Sheriff Cantwell.

"I thought you had an officer guarding Mrs. Reedman, what happened?"

"Officer Pohs had to leave for a while, She'd just left when she heard the shots fired followed by an explosion and the fire. I'm on my way out there right now. You can meet me there."

Jack quickly told his wife where he was going before making his way out to the cruiser parked in front of the house. In the past, several people criticized him for taking the squad car home. Tonight, he was glad he'd flown in the face of public opinion.

He drove through town at top speed with sirens and lights going. By the time the firefighters were knocking down the flames engulfing the house where, if memory served him right, the library sat. Many years ago, he'd been to a party here and remembered the layout of the mansion. He prayed he'd be able to salvage the phone and answering machine. He wanted to hear the messages for himself. At the same time, he wondered how he was going to pull off the ruse about Kitty Reedman being dead.

More sirens cut through the silence of the night and Jack looked up to see at least three county squads enter the circular driveway.

"I don't like all this secrecy," Sheriff Cantwell greeted him. "Where is your officer?"

At this point, he knew he couldn't pull this off without letting the sheriff in on everything. Reluctantly, Jack filled

Sheriff Cantwell in on everything Rhonda told him earlier.

"Officer Pohs thinks it's best if we put out a press release saying Mrs. Reedman was killed tonight."

"Where is Officer Pohs?" Cantwell pressed, obviously upset with getting the information second hand.

"Officer Pohs assures me they're both safe, but she wouldn't tell me where. I'm just hoping the department gets this fire knocked down fast enough to save the answering machine. There should be two very incriminating messages on it."

~ * ~

Rhonda closed her eyes and tried to comprehend what all transpired tonight. She thanked God she'd sent Kitty off in the cruiser. If Kitty heard the last message, she might have panicked and not made it out of the house. Instead of pretending to be dead, her death could have been for real.

"I can't believe someone set the house on fire."

Kitty's voice cut into Rhonda's thoughts.

"Look at it this way," Rhonda replied. "At least they gave you enough warning so you could get out. We were lucky the ruse worked. If things go as I planned, it will be reported that authorities found you dead in the house."

"What about Karl's kids? They could be the next targets. It sounds as though these people seem to think they deserve the money from Karl's estate. The way I see it, with me out of the way only his kids are standing between them and the money."

Rhonda nodded, knowing full well Kitty couldn't see her do so in the dark. She'd completely underestimated Kitty. So much happened in the last two hours, Rhonda hadn't given Karl's kids a thought. It was apparent Kitty had been thinking of them. Even though she didn't want to talk to Jack, she knew she had to give him a heads-up about Brad and Donna.

Calling his number, she waited for him to answer.

"Where are you," he asked when he answered her call.

"That doesn't matter. Whoever is doing this thinks Kitty will inherit Karl's money. For some warped reason, they think they should get it rather than Kitty or anyone else in the family. You should think about guarding Karl's kids."

"I'll pass the word onto the sheriff. I just wish you'd let me know where you are."

"Look, for all intents and purposes, Kitty Reedman is in the morgue."

Completely exasperated, Rhonda ended the call and turned off the ringer.

"I take it you were talking to Jack."

Mark obviously scrutinized the frown on her face in the light from the headlights of an oncoming car.

"You take it right. Jack has his days, but today isn't one of them."

"So, does this mean I'm officially dead?" Kitty asked from the back seat.

"That's right. For all intents and purposes, you're dead until we can find out who is behind this. If you think of anything, no matter how trivial, be sure to let me know right away."

Before going out to the cottage, Mark stopped at the twenty-four-hour convenience store on the highway. Leaving Kitty in the car, Mark and Rhonda went inside.

"Hi, Mark," the clerk greeted him. "Didn't expect to see anyone up here with your folks out of town and all."

"Rhonda's busy with a big case back home, so I decided to come up and do some fishing. Her car is in the shop, so when her shift ended, she drove me up. That way she'll have the SUV and not be stranded."

"I told Mark, I could catch a ride with someone, but he insisted. I know how much he likes his fishing. If he's out on the lake the last thing on his mind will be driving. I insisted we at least stock the pantry in case the fish aren't biting."

"Big case, you say," the clerk commented, as though he hadn't heard anything Rhonda said. "Is it the guy who got his pecker cut off and was thrown in the lake? I've been hearing all about it on the news. I was pretty sure it happened in the town where you worked on the police force. I can't believe they'd have a woman on someone that big."

"Well, they do."

Rhonda bit her tongue to keep from giving the guy a tongue-lashing he wouldn't soon forget. Without saying more, she watched as Mark picked up staples like bread, milk, coffee, eggs, and bacon, knowing full well the freezer and cupboards would be well-stocked. Mark put everything down on the counter and made small talk before going out to fill the vehicle with gas while Rhonda paid the bill.

They stopped there every time they came up to the cottage during the summer. It certainly wasn't unusual for Rhonda to bring Mark up, then go back to town. With his schedule free when school wasn't in session, he had ample opportunity to indulge in his favorite summer pastime while she was working.

By the time they arrived at the cottage, Rhonda knew she wouldn't be driving back tonight. With everything they had been through over the past few hours she was too exhausted to feel safe on the road.

Chapter Six

Jack paced his office. He wondered if Rhonda would come in to work today. Her shift was due to start in ten minutes and she was nowhere in sight.

He caught a glimpse of her SUV pulling into the parking lot at the same time Sheriff Cantwell parked his vehicle.

Rhonda parked her SUV in the employee's lot, while the sheriff pulled into the space at the front door. His choice of parking places annoyed Jack no end. The man could certainly use the exercise to work off the number of donuts he consumed every time he came to the office.

"I've got some more information on our case," Sheriff Cantwell announced once he entered Jack's office. "What I have blows the theory by your lady cop right out of the water."

He tapped the manila envelope he carried against his free hand for emphasis.

Before commenting, Jack saw Rhonda enter the office and motioned for her to join them. "Officer Pohs, this is Sheriff Cantwell," he said, making the proper introductions.

He watched Rhonda hold out her hand and wait a few moments for Sheriff Cantwell to do likewise. When he shifted the envelope from hand to hand, she withdrew her offer to shake hands.

Jack finally broke the awkward silence hanging between Rhonda and the sheriff. "Sheriff Cantwell tells me; he has some new information regarding our case."

"New information?" Rhonda questioned.

"Yes. The lab just finished with the victim's...ah...his..."

"The word is penis," Rhonda added, saying the word the

sheriff seemed too embarrassed to utter.

"Yeah, that. Anyway, they took DNA from it and this dude wasn't exactly clean. There were four DNA samples, all from women. The way I see it, there were four females responsible for this murder. There are still some more tests that need to be run, but at least this gives us something new to go on."

"New?" Jack echoed. "How in the hell could there be four?"

"Like I said, the lab is still sorting all of that out, we figure two of them are Mrs. Reedman and Ms. Barclay. Since we don't know where the grieving widow is, we can't get a DNA sample from her, but we can get one from Ms. Barclay. To be truthful, I don't like this business of pretending Kitty Reedman is dead, I don't know what you think you'll prove by it."

"Look Cantwell," Jack said, 'I agree with Rhonda on this one. Whoever is behind this wants Kitty dead. Why else would he have fired shots into the house before he threw in the firebomb?"

"It still doesn't make any sense to me, but since the news has been reported on the radio and TV, I certainly can't come out and say otherwise. My money is on whose DNA is on this poor bastard's dick."

~ * ~

For the second time in less than twenty-four hours, Rhonda bit her tongue until she thought it would bleed. More than anything else in the world, she wanted to shout that the threatening phone calls certainly weren't from a woman. From the way both Jack and Sheriff Cantwell acted, she didn't expect either of them to be receptive to anything she had to say.

Cantwell continued with his speculations, saying the

fact Karl had been with four different women since he last showered said the murderers had to be female.

Rhonda completely disagreed, but kept her mouth shut. She just wanted him to leave, so Jack could fill her in on what happened at the Reedman mansion last night.

After half an hour, Sheriff Cantwell left the envelope he'd carried earlier in Jack's care and left to go back to his office.

"So, I don't suppose you want to tell me where you have Kitty stashed," Jack began.

"No, but I do want to know what went on last night. I heard shots and breaking glass before the explosion. The news was sketchy, but it did report Kitty's death."

"Your trigger-happy friend probably shot out the window in the library, then threw the firebomb. There was a lot of damage to the library as well as the dining room. I couldn't get the phone."

Rhonda nodded. "I have the old one in the car. When I hooked up the new one, I saw there was a mailbox within the phone, as well as a back-up the phone company provides. We should be able to get the messages from them."

"Between the two phones, there are over thirty messages you should hear."

"Well, that's a relief. If these messages are as bad as you say they are, it looks like we're going to be building quite a solid case. What do you make of this business of the DNA samples?"

"I don't know. What I do know is that Kitty wasn't in on this. If she were, she wouldn't have someone harassing her and shooting at the house, to say nothing about setting it on fire. I can get you a sample from Kitty, but I don't think it will do you any good. When I asked her what went on the day of the murder, she said she and Suzie were planning a threesome with Karl, but Suzie got called into work. I doubt Karl and Kitty had sex before he went out to get cigarettes."

~ * ~

Rhonda left the office and headed for her patrol car. Even though she left Jack the tapes of the messages Kitty had been receiving, that didn't mean he would listen to them. He was stuck on the DNA report. She wished she could get a look at it, but considering her position with the department, she had a better chance of being promoted to chief than to see the report. Being one of the newest officers on the force, she was low man on the totem pole, so to say. It was one thing for Jack to give her the job of guarding Kitty Reedman, but it was another for him to allow her access to anything pertaining to the investigation.

After pulling out of the parking lot, she headed toward the Reedman mansion to see for herself the damage done by last night's firebombing. It would have been out of her jurisdiction if the city hadn't annexed the land surrounding the mansion two years ago. Today, she had no reason not to be on the road heading out there.

The entire center section of the house was burned to the ground, but the east wing housing the kitchen and laundry area, as well as the west wing where the bedrooms were located, stood intact. It was as though someone plucked the center out of the home leaving the two sides to stand on their own. There would be smoke and water damage to the area, but otherwise they could remain, that is if Donna decided to rebuild the living room, dining room and the library. The basement was a total loss including the swimming pool located directly beneath the family room. Whoever bombed the house and fired the shots must have stood across the driveway. With the number of cars and trucks responding to last night's disaster any trace of tracks or any evidence left by the arsonists would have been obliterated.

After stepping under the yellow crime scene tape, she

examined the charred remains. There was nothing left to say how the fire started, but she heard the explosion, even if no one else did.

A moment later, she noticed something reflecting in the morning sunlight. After pulling on a pair of gloves, she bent over to pick up a shard of glass. It didn't look as though it belonged there. Instead, she recognized it as a piece from a bottle. That wasn't as incriminating as the fact it was hard to buy things in glass anymore. When she went to the grocery store, she found mustard, ketchup, soda and even vinegar in plastic bottles. It was getting harder and harder to find anything packaged in glass.

She returned to the car for an evidence bag. Putting the pieces of glass, she was now uncovering into the bag. She continued to look through the rubble. There was only a small portion of the bombed-out area where she was able to walk, since most of the contents of the library fell into the basement during the fire.

With as much of the evidence as she could gather in the bag, she walked around to the back of the house and into the exposed basement. Remnants of the dining room and library filled the indoor swimming pool. In the mess she could see shards of the dishes they'd used for dinner the night before. Memories of the small talk they'd made in the face of the danger lurking just minutes away filled her mind.

Mixed with the broken china, she found more pieces of the same kind of glass from upstairs. It was obvious someone made a bottle bomb like the ones she'd read about in the various mysteries she'd enjoyed over the years. In those stories, they were referred to as Molotov cocktails. She doubted the same people who were making the threatening calls would have the skill to make something so deadly, but anything was possible. From what she'd read anyone could learn how to make a bomb off the Internet these days.

She was just about ready to leave the mansion and

return to the office with what she found, when her cell phone rang. Checking the number, she saw Chief Franks' number on the caller ID.

"Rhonda," he said as soon as she answered. "I need you to go over to Donna Kelly's house."

The fact he called rather than make radio contact came as a surprise. "Why? What happened?"

"She just called in and said she's been getting some harassing phone calls ever since the fire last night. I want you to go over there and investigate. I figured you have some experience with this kind of thing and besides, Donna would trust you more than she would any of the male officers. Somehow, she seems to know you were guarding Kitty last night when all the trouble started."

Rhonda sighed deeply. Jack was trying to put the blame for Kitty's supposed death onto her shoulders and she would have to try and explain things to Donna without giving away the fact Kitty hadn't died or her whereabouts.

"I'll get right over there. What about Brad?"

"We haven't heard from him, but I do know he's staying at Donna's place, since he lives out of state. You can kill two birds with one stone by going over there."

Rhonda didn't appreciate Jack's choice of words but refused to comment on it and get into an argument with her boss. Just as she ended the call, something else caught her eye. In the middle of the rubble rested a floor safe she didn't know existed. Before leaving the property, she made a mental note to have someone return and retrieve it. If they were lucky, it could yield some clue as to who was behind the murder of Karl, the firebombing, and the attempted murder of Kitty.

As she drove toward Donna's home, she wondered what she would say to Karl's daughter as well as his son. It was her job to protect Kitty, but would they blame her for what everyone thought to be their stepmother's murder?

It took about ten minutes for Rhonda to drive from the

mansion to Donna's elaborate home on the west side of town. Donna's husband, Sean Kelly, answered the door almost before Rhonda took her finger from the doorbell button.

From the look on his face, Rhonda knew this wasn't going to be a pleasant visit by any stretch of the imagination. He didn't say anything but did take a step aside so she could enter the living room of the house.

"I can't believe they sent you," Brad Reedman spat as soon as he saw her. "If you'd done your job, Kitty would still be alive. How could you leave her in that house when you knew people were threatening her life?"

Rhonda pondered her answer for a moment. In order to get these people to trust her, she knew she should tell them the truth, but something in her mind told her it was best if she made up a believable lie.

Before she could begin, the phone rang, and Donna's expression mirrored her panic.

"Let your answering machine pick up," Rhonda cautioned, "If it's someone you want to talk to you can always answer it yourself."

The message left by Sean before any of this happened came on and Rhonda held her breath. It took only a moment for a now familiar voice to leave a message just as threatening as any she'd heard while staying with Kitty.

"Is that the voice of the person who called earlier?" she asked, once the message finished.

Donna shook her head no. "This is the third call and the third different voice, what do they want? Will they try to kill us the way they did Kitty?"

Rhonda knew she didn't have an answer to the question Donna posed. "I don't know. Kitty was getting the same type of phone calls. They started on Sunday and intensified by last night. We have copies of all the calls at the station and we've been listening to them. That's why I discouraged you from picking up the phone when it rang just now. The last message

Kitty received just before the firebombing was extremely nasty. That was when I decided I had to get Kitty out of harm's way."

"Then she isn't dead?" Donna gasped.

"I didn't say that. Between the two of us, we decided she had to leave the house. I wanted to take her with me in the squad car, but she insisted there were some things she wanted to take with her. Reluctantly, I agreed she could stay long enough to get her things and meet me in town. By the time I got back to the station the report of the firebombing came in. Believe me, I blame myself as much as you blame me, but this was a decision the two of us made together. Unfortunately, it was the wrong decision, but I can't change the past."

"I can understand the position you were put in. It couldn't have been an easy decision to make, but of course, you had no idea what these people were capable of doing," Sean commented.

"Whoever is involved seems to think they can lay claim to Karl's fortune. Do you have any idea who might feel that way? If you have any thoughts on the subject, let me know right away. At this point the four of you are in as much danger as your father and Kitty were."

Brad shook his head. "If there is someone, I doubt I'd know anything about it. The old man and I weren't exactly on speaking terms. That's the reason he sent me to Denver to run the office there. He didn't like me selling siding when we had a business in Denver that needed me. We never could be in the same office, to say nothing of the same town together. Did he say anything to you, Sis?"

"Hardly. I had my hands full trying to get Daddy to agree a bed and breakfast would be the perfect use for the mansion, when and if he were to pass away. It wasn't like we were pushing to start it up, but we thought it would be a great investment for our retirement."

Rhonda filed this new information away in her mind.

From what Kitty said, she thought Donna's idea of a bed and breakfast at the mansion met with Karl's approval. Either Kitty was sugarcoating things, or Karl hadn't voiced his opposition in her presence. She was willing to bet the truth lay in the latter option. Having known Karl Reedman's reputation, she realized he probably didn't confide in his wives in the same way other husbands did.

"Do you think someone will try to take our lives?" Brad asked.

"It's entirely possible. To be on the safe side, I'd like to suggest we find someplace where you can stay until we decide who is behind this. You have to be at the visitation tonight and the funeral tomorrow, but I do think you need to go somewhere more secure."

"Won't we be followed?" Sean inquired.

"I've been thinking about that. You should be all right until it's time to go to the funeral home. It's best if you all go together. Afterward, someone from the department will take you to a safe house. I'll bring your car back here and at the same time, I'll put your lights on a timer. If they plan to do anything, it will be after the visitation tonight, I'm prepared to stay here, and house sit for you. The only difference is this time we'll have other officers here with me."

Even though she hadn't run the plan past either Jack of the sheriff, she felt certain it would work.

~ * ~

"You want to do what?" Jack shouted into the phone. "You put your life on the line last night. I don't think you should be doing it again."

"Who better than me?" Rhonda replied. "I know how these characters work. They'll be watching at the visitation for the family to leave and go home before they make any moves."

"You don't even know if they're going to do anything

tonight. How is that husband of yours going to react to your staying at the Kelly house with three sheriff's deputies?"

"Don't worry about Mark. He'll be just fine without me. In the meantime, maybe you should offer some protection to Susan Barclay. She's been involved with Karl, too. I doubt she's in any danger, but you do need to get a DNA sample from her. It would be for the best if you did it while someone was guarding her. If she turns down the offer, so be it."

Jack nodded his head as though she could hear his agreement without him verbally giving it. "That might be a good idea," he finally said. "I do have to admit, I've been thinking about it, but we haven't been able to locate the lovely Ms. Barclay. It appears she fell off the face of the earth. You wouldn't have any ideas about where we might find her, would you?"

"If she's smart, she's out of town until this whole thing is resolved. With Karl being murdered and the news reporting Kitty's murder, she might think she's next. I'll ask Kitty where she might have gone, but I doubt I'll learn anything."

Jack hung up the phone. Rhonda was certainly overstepping her bounds, but he knew she felt responsible for what happened to the Reedman family, since Kitty's house had been firebombed while Rhonda acted as a bodyguard for Kitty.

Earlier in the conversation Rhonda mentioned the floor safe that now resided at the bottom of the indoor pool with the rest of the rubble from the upper floor. If it were immersed in water, what would the condition of the contents be?

Without giving the matter further thought, he placed a call to the sheriff's office. The least he could do would be get Rhonda some back-up for tonight. If the murderers were watching the Kelly house, they'd be expecting a car to come back after the visitation with four people in it.

Jack considered himself lucky to have the sheriff be receptive to Rhonda's idea. It came as a surprise, since when they first met, he was less than excited about Jack's lone female officer. Even though there were females on the county force, this guy was the epidemy of a male chauvinist pig. His comment after first meeting Rhonda, had been he thought she'd be better walking the streets rather than protecting them.

Before going back out to the scene of the fire, Jack arranged for Donna and Sean as well as Brad and Lorette to stay at a secure location until Rhonda felt it safe for them to return to Donna and Sean's home.

Chapter Seven

Not wanting to leave Karl's kids alone, Rhonda borrowed a black dress from Donna. Like Kitty, they were about the same size with matching hair color.

"I can't believe Kitty is dead," Donna said, while they got dressed.

Rhonda noticed tears in Donna's green eyes. As much as she wanted to tell Donna the truth, she refrained. It was better for Donna to think the worst and be on guard.

"I'm afraid so. Hopefully, I'll get some vibes off someone at either the visitation tonight or the funeral tomorrow. My job is not only to find out who is behind this, but also to keep you and your family safe."

"What about my father's other wives? I know Mom is in Florida, Marie is in California, but Christine is in Madison. Is she safe?"

"I doubt the killers think the ex-wives are a threat to them. They seem to want a share of your father's money. Up until last night, it was Kitty they thought was standing between them and their ideas about getting it. With her out of the way you and Brad are the next logical targets."

As soon as she spoke the words, Rhonda regretted them. There was no need to frighten Karl's kids any more than necessary. On the other hand, their lives were in danger and ignorance could be deadly.

"I'm glad you're being up front with me," Donna said. "If you're ready to go, I'll check with everyone else."

Rhonda nodded. She needed to call Mark and fill him in on what was going on. She hated putting her husband in the middle of something like this but didn't have any other choice.

Someone had to look after Kitty and Rhonda knew Mark would protect her with his life.

She waited until Donna left the room before placing the call to Mark.

"How's it going?" he greeted her.

"To quote Alice in Wonderland, it just gets curiouser and curiouser. I won't be coming up to be with you tonight."

"Why not?" Mark questioned, concern sounding in his voice.

"Babysitting duty. This time it's Brad and Donna who are getting the calls. I don't want Kitty to know about it though."

"I don't like you being alone in such a situation. Remember what happened last night. Do you want me to come down and be with you?"

"That won't be necessary. It's more important for you to stay where you are. Besides, I have back-up coming from both the city and the county."

"Should I be worried about you with all those men?" he teased.

"Hardly. It will be two male officers, a female and me. I think I'll be quite safe. Can I speak to Kitty?"

Rhonda waited while Mark handed his phone to Kitty. It seemed strange for him to be jealous of her with other officers when she trusted him completely with Kitty.

"I wish I could be there for the visitation tonight," Kitty said as soon as she answered the phone. It was evident she'd been crying. "Are you going?"

"You know I am. I have a question to ask you before we leave. Did you and Karl have sex on the day he was killed?"

"Of course, we did. We always did first thing in the morning before we'd shower together. Like I told you when this first happened, we were planning on having a threesome later that night. By the time Karl went out for cigarettes we both knew Suzie wasn't coming. We were planning to have shrimp and wine when he got home just to set the mood for our own pleasure later in the evening."

Rhonda recalled seeing the wine as well as the plate of shrimp in the kitchen when she investigated the morning after the murder. Kitty mentioned it and showed her the untouched shrimp plate she'd taken to the kitchen for disposal. From the aroma wafting from it, Rhonda knew it had been sitting out too long.

"I sense there's something you aren't telling me," Kitty complained.

"It's just something the county came up with in their investigation. I'm not at liberty to say anything more. Are you enjoying the lake?"

She hoped the change of subject would help to lighten the situation. The last thing she needed was for Kitty to find out about either the four female DNAs found on her husband's penis, or the calls Donna was receiving.

She listened as Kitty described swimming and enjoying the fresh fish Mark caught for dinner. At least with everyone thinking Kitty was dead, being so many miles away from town would keep her safe.

"How badly burned is the house? Will Donna be able to rebuild it for the bed and breakfast?"

Kitty's question surprised Rhonda. It was becoming increasingly apparent Kitty had a strong bond with her stepchildren.

"The damage was contained to the center portion of the house. Unfortunately, the library, family room and dining room are now littering the pool in the basement."

Kitty groaned. It probably wasn't fair to tell her, but she'd find out anyway. With a case of this magnitude, the state papers would pick up the story and run pictures of the fire damage in their morning editions.

"What about the floor safe?" Kitty asked.

"I found it in the rubble. I called Jack and asked him to

arrange to go out and pick it up. Do you know the combination?"

"Hardly. Karl guarded the combination like it was a state secret. He told me he kept important papers there until he could transfer them to the safety deposit box at the bank. In all the excitement, I forgot all about it. If someone can get it open, maybe there is something inside that could help with the investigation."

"Does anyone else have the combination?"

Kitty waited a long moment before answering. "I doubt it. At one time I heard Karl telling Brad and Donna about it, but he said the combination was none of their business. They weren't happy about it, but they said they understood. I think they thought he might keep money in there and were worried about someone finding out about it."

~ * ~

Rhonda cursed the heels she wore to the visitation. Thank goodness she found a chair where she could scrutinize the line of people paying their respects to the family.

As expected, the town leaders were some of the first in line. It seemed almost laughable to see them there, since Karl either had affairs with their wives or propositioned them.

It was easy to spot the curiosity seekers. They offered the family limp-fish handshakes, as well as hollow words of condolence.

Scattered among the mourners were several young couples. Rhonda figured they were friends of either Donna or Brad. For some reason, she watched them as they made their way through the line. The first two couples stood several feet from the second two as though they were purposely trying to put distance between themselves.

For some unknow reason, she watched the first two couples as they made their way through the long line. Only the morbidly curious or those truly wanting to express their sympathy stuck it out. These people didn't seem to be in either category. They looked as though they thought being there was a necessary evil.

Rhonda kept an eye on them while monitoring the conversations of the other people in line. It never ceased to amaze her as to the conversations one could hear while eavesdropping on the people waiting in line to greet the family.

The comment voiced the most was that the closed casket surprised people. Knowing the extent of Karl's injuries, it was absurd to even consider trying to make him presentable for showing. Rhonda chalked the comments up to morbid curiosity.

"Ain't it a shame about his wife being killed?"

Rhonda listened more intently. This was the first time Kitty's reported death was mentioned within her hearing. She glanced up to see the first two young people standing across from where she was sitting.

"It certainly is," one of the women said. "I mean everyone knew that old man was a horny bastard, but I never heard anything bad about his wife. She did a lot of volunteer work at the hospital. I work in pediatrics and the kids loved it when she came to read to them."

"From what I hear, it was all show," the first man who spoke said. "You know a way to get her face in the paper. These high mucky mucks with more money than brains piss me off. Sure, it's all fine and good to give money to the hospital, but what about the rest of us? In this economy wouldn't the funds be better used for the everyday working stiff?"

The line moved on and Rhonda picked up on another conversation. Taking a note pad from her purse, she jotted down the names of the people in front and behind the two couples. They were both well-known people from town. If the strangers signed the guest book, she'd be able to get their names.

With many more conversations swirling around her, Rhonda kept an eye on the first two young couples in line. By the time they reached Donna, Rhonda looked for any sign of recognition. Donna's blank look spoke silent volumes. She didn't have to be a genius to know neither Donna nor Brad knew these people.

Donna nodded as she shook hands with the two men and one of the women. When the second woman stepped up to where Donna stood, she didn't shake hands. Instead, she embraced Donna, whose reaction was obviously without emotion, as though a stranger was embracing her.

Earlier, she saw Jack go through the line, so when he took the seat next to her, it came as no surprise.

"Are you here for the duration?" he questioned.

"I'm afraid so. I'm certain you're aware of the plan." She tried to keep her voice low.

Jack nodded, then glanced toward the door. Rhonda followed his gaze and saw Officer Roberts enter the room.

"He'll be with you," Jack commented.

Rhonda was pleased with Jack's choice of officers. Paul Roberts was the youngest member of the department, making him much closer to the ages of the people they would be protecting. Until he joined the force, she'd been the one with the least seniority.

"Guess I should take off. I can see the wife at the door tapping her foot. You know how women are when us men are off doing our own thing."

Inside, Rhonda seethed, though she agreed with him. Not only was Jack well known in the community, but with him sitting next to her, she was unable to monitor the conversations going on around her.

In a way, she envied Jack being able to go home with his wife and stay completely out of danger, while she would be at the mercy of the people who killed Karl and thought they killed Kitty. As the chief of police, he could sit back and give orders without putting himself in jeopardy.

~ * ~

It was almost ten when the last of the visitors went through the line. Brad and Donna looked exhausted and with good reason. They'd arrived at three and been receiving condolences for six hours straight.

Once everyone left, the family was ushered out the back to a waiting van, leaving Paul, Rhonda and the two county officers to walk through the darkened front lot to get into Brad's car. In the car, Deputy Alice Knight and Deputy Steve Kline introduced themselves. The two were great choices, as in the dark they could easily be mistaken for Brad's wife and Donna's husband.

"So, I hear we're husband and wife for the night," Steve said, his hand wandering to Rhonda's knee.

"In name only," she reminded him, pushing his hand from her knee. "You'll be bunking with Paul in the guest bedroom, while Alice and I will be in the master bedroom."

"You've been on this case from the beginning," Alice commented. "Do you expect any trouble?"

Rhonda thought about her response. "The calls at the mansion started on Sunday and got worse on Monday. The shots fired and the firebombing came on Monday night. If they're true to form, there should be something going on either tonight or maybe tomorrow after the funeral."

"Do you have any suspects?" Steve questioned.

"We have a whole town full of them. Karl Reedman was not a well-liked man."

"You could have fooled me," Steve continued. "I've never seen such a large visitation in my life."

"I was watching the people going through the line. Most

of the people there came because they felt they had to or else they were curiosity seekers. A lot of people were disappointed about it being a closed casket."

"If that's the case, why did they stay?"

"I can tell you're not from a small town. They stayed because they wanted to be seen paying their respects to the family. It's a social thing."

Donna's house came into view, stopping their conversation. On the street there were no parked cars, which Rhonda decided was a good thing. She could breathe a sigh of relief once the garage door closed behind them.

"I didn't want to frighten you, but we were followed all the way from the funeral home," Paul advised them.

Rhonda felt a shiver of dread make its way down her spine. She didn't know if the two couples she'd observed earlier were involved, but it bothered her all the same. Even more upsetting was the fact Jack monopolized her attention and the other two couples went through the line without her being able to monitor their conversation.

They no more than turned on the lights in the house than the phone rang. Steve reached for it, but Rhonda stopped him. "Let the machine pick up this call," she cautioned.

"Didn't think the visitation would ever get over. It was amazing the number of friends the old bastard had. With his whore out of the way that leaves you two with all the money. Don't think you'll ever get to spend it."

A loud click indicated the end of the message.

"Are they all like that?" Alice questioned.

Rhonda nodded. "This one is relatively mild. I doubt there were any while we were gone, but it's worth listening to them to make sure."

To her surprise three new messages, one from each of the voices she was now so familiar with, were on the machine. Unlike the one just left, these were more profane and more threatening.

"Were these the kind of calls Mrs. Reedman was getting before her death?"

"I'm afraid they are."

"If that's so, why did you leave her alone?"

Steve's question hit her hard. Rhonda practiced the answer she and Jack had devised, and it still sounded lame. "We were working on a plan to get her to a safe house. We never thought they would be watching the house so closely. She was killed in the firebombing minutes after we left."

"Who do you mean by we?"

"My husband joined us. I left to take the cruiser back to the office and he was to meet Kitty on the road that runs behind the house. That was the way Jack planned it."

"It makes you wonder what the top brass was thinking of," Alice said sarcastically. "If you hadn't followed orders, Mrs. Reedman would still be alive, and you'd probably be up for disciplinary action. It just doesn't make sense to me. Maybe when I have more seniority, I might be more understanding of it all. For now, it's nothing more than a lot of B.S."

"As late as it's getting, I think we should all get some rest," Paul suggested. "I don't think the girls should share the master bedroom, though."

"Why not?" Rhonda questioned, not able to quite understand his meaning.

"Because if Donna is their next target, it stands to reason the people behind this have checked out this house. It would be perfectly normal for Donna and her husband to go to bed in their room. I think we should turn on the lights, like they're getting ready for bed, then turn them off. I've been looking the house over and there are four bedrooms here. It makes sense for Rhonda, Alice and one of us guys to stay in the guest bedrooms. I also think we should keep watch on the street. I'll take the first shift, then wake Alice at two to relieve me. She can get Steve up at four to take over."

"What about me?" Rhonda asked.

"From what I can see, you look completely exhausted. Of all of us, you're the one who could use a good night's sleep. I don't think this will be over after the funeral. If that's the case, you'll need all the rest you can get."

"I tend to agree with the kid," Steve said. "After what you went through last night, you deserve to get some rest."

Rhonda nodded. It had been well past midnight when they finally got to bed last night, and she'd gotten up at four this morning in order to make the two-hour drive back to town and be at work by seven. Added to that, the threats to Brad and Donna seemed to take an emotional toll on her as well.

Without protest, she headed toward one of the guest bedrooms. The one she chose was painted a delicate shade of pink and looked very Victorian. As she snuggled under the down comforter, she closed her eyes. Instead of the instant sleep she so craved, her mind whirled with the conversations she'd overheard at the funeral home.

The young man at the funeral home referred to Karl as an old bastard, just as the caller had when they first arrived at the house. Unfortunately, the voice of the man she heard tonight was an unfamiliar one. It was far too deep to be any of the callers and she knew disguising a deep bass like his would be next to impossible. Until she could see the guest book and check out who those people were, she had no leads whatsoever.

Chapter Eight

The aroma of freshly made coffee combined with the chiming of the clock in the living room woke Rhonda. She couldn't believe she'd slept so late and so soundly. The clock on the bedside table confirmed it was eight in the morning.

Getting out of bed, she put on the robe she'd borrowed from Donna's closet and hurried toward the bathroom. Once she finished her morning ritual, she found her three companions waiting in the kitchen.

"How did last night go?" she asked.

"Only a couple more calls after midnight, but other than the car that was following us earlier going past the house, nothing," Paul advised her.

"Are you sure it was the same car that was following us?"

"Positive. I got a good look at it in the rearview mirror. It's a silver or grey Chevy Impala. I couldn't read the license plate, though."

"Any idea how old this vehicle is?" Steve asked.

"It's hard to tell. You know all these new models look a lot alike, especially in the dark. If my folks didn't drive an Impala, I probably wouldn't have known as much as I do about the model."

Rhonda grabbed a cup of coffee and a slice of toast. It would take a while for both her and Alice to get ready to go to the church and be there prior to ten. There was little time to waste on eating breakfast.

~ * ~

The church, like the funeral home, was packed. Rhonda and her companions sat inconspicuously in the back and watched as the mourners again passed the casket. The somber looks on their faces said the insincerity of last night had been replaced by the reality of the fact a member of their community had been brutally murdered.

Behind Brad and Donna, sat all three of Karl's former wives. No matter what he put them through with his affairs, they all cried openly. Adding to the unlikely mix of mourners were the television cameras, catching everything for posterity and the evening news.

The cameras panned the church, until the minister asked them not to film the service.

Once the funeral ended, the television cameras again began filming, catching the expressions of all the mourners for the six o'clock news. As they prearranged, Rhonda and her fellow officers left the church before the family. Fearing an unexpected attack, they shielded the family from anything that might happen.

Rhonda walked in front of Donna, while each of the other officers shielded the family members, they were impersonating the night before. She didn't see the rock until she felt it hit her forehead. As she pitched forward, it was Paul who reacted quickly enough to catch her. She was aware of the panicked conversations as well as the movement behind her and the cameras recording every drop of blood falling from the gash left by the rock that hit her.

"Someone already called for an ambulance," Paul informed her.

"That's unnecessary," she protested. "I'm sure it's just a little nick. I'm fine and…"

"…and nothing. I want you checked out."

She looked up, surprised to see Jack at her side. The blurriness of her vision came as a surprise.

"I assure you; I am all right. I've gotten worse mosquito

61

bites in my backyard."

She knew the words sounded hollow, but they were the ones she felt obligated to voice.

Sirens screamed from every direction and the steps of the church swarmed with emergency personnel. Although Rhonda wanted to ask about Brad and Donna, she knew she would never be heard over the commotion.

Rhonda put her hand to her injured head and felt the sticky wetness of blood. Before she could investigate the wound further, one of the EMT's knelt beside her and gently put her hand down to her side.

"Head wounds bleed profusely," he cautioned. "To avoid infection, it's best if you don't touch it. We'll get it covered, then transport you to the hospital."

"It that necessary? I have to protect Brad and Donna," she protested, as he put a cervical collar on her neck and transferred to a backboard before putting her on a gurney.

"We'll take care of it," Jack assured her.

Rhonda closed her eyes and resigned herself to the mandatory trip to the hospital. With the number of officers on the scene, Brad and Donna would be well protected.

~ * ~

Once the ambulance pulled away from the church, Jack noticed a small rock lying next to where Rhonda fell. From the traces of blood on it, he realized someone must have used a slingshot to propel it toward Rhonda. He wondered if it was meant for her or if their aim was off and they were trying to injure Brad or Donna.

"What do you make of this?" Jack asked the sheriff, holding out the plastic bag containing the rock once they were in the basement of the church for the luncheon.

"I can't believe the people behind this would use a rock and a slingshot. It's more likely kids with too much time on their hands. The people we're looking for are much too sophisticated to use such a primitive weapon."

For once, Jack didn't argue with the sheriff, but kept his opinions to himself. "At least the family is safe. I need to talk to Brad and Donna. Getting away from here as soon as possible might not be such a bad idea."

"I agree with you there. Since they've been getting phone calls, it might be for the best if they did leave town for a while. Of course, Brad can go home, but Donna has to stay here. We certainly don't need anyone else killed over this. I talked to my officers earlier. They said there were several calls last night and they were followed when they went back to the house. I don't like the way this is shaping up. Considering the information we have, there were certainly women involved in this murder. Whoever they are, they're more sophisticated than I gave them credit for being."

Jack saw Brad and Donna finish going through the line together for the buffet. Seeing brother and sister together, he remembered them as children. At the time both of their mothers were still living in town and not far from each other either. Every morning Brad went over to walk Donna to the grade school before going next door to the junior high. The parents in town remarked about it being an excellent idea to have all the schools in one central location. In that way, the older kids could look after the younger ones. It now seemed Brad was still trying to look after his sister, but in this matter, they were both in trouble.

Once they were seated at the table reserved for them, Jack went to sit at the same table. Their expressions were hard to read. Of course, there was grief and fear, but he also detected concern.

"What happened earlier?" Brad asked as soon as Jack joined them. "Will Rhonda be all right?"

"I'm sure she will. You know how head wounds are, they bleed like crazy, but they usually aren't life threatening.

I mean, this isn't David slaying Goliath in Biblical times. The only comparison is the assailant must have used a slingshot to throw the rock at her. At least that's what I think happened. She has a good-sized cut on her forehead, but after she gets some stitches and rests she should be as good as new. I sent one of my officers to the hospital with her. I tend to agree with the sheriff that it was probably kids lobbing rocks for kicks."

Even though he didn't completely agree with the sheriff, he felt it best to keep that information from Brad and Donna.

"We're considering going away for a few days," Sean's voice was so low, only the people at their table could hear. "Do you think Rhonda and Paul could stay at our house to monitor the calls?"

Jack marveled at the fact Sean suggested the same thing he came over to the table to talk to them about.

"What about you and Loretta, Brad?" Jack asked.

"We agree with Donna and Sean. This could get ugly. Whoever these people are, they seem intent on getting rid of anybody connected with Dad. We've been talking about going to Chicago this afternoon and booking a flight to Aruba. Sean has a friend with a condo down there. He said we can use it whenever we want."

Jack nodded. He looked around the room and found Colin Masters. He was the only person around who had the means to have a condo on a secluded island paradise. Since Sean and Colin had been best friends all through their school years, it was only natural for him to offer them a place to get away.

It was all fine and good for the Reedman kids to want to get away, but he deeply resented Sean's suggestion he put Rhonda in further danger. Of course, it only made sense. Rhonda was familiar with the case and, hopefully, there wouldn't be any reason for her to be hospitalized once the stiches were in place. Even though it made sense, he wanted her on the case and not stuck in the hospital making herself a royal pain in the ass. As a matter of fact, staying at the Kelly house would get her out of his hair for a few days, giving her the rest, she needed. "I think that could be arranged, depending on what the doctors at the hospital say."

"We'd be forever grateful," Brad commented. "Rhonda has been on top of things where we're concerned. I do hope she'll be recognized for her efforts."

The comment made Jack's blood boil. As far as he was concerned, Rhonda was a thorn in his side. It didn't help she'd taken on the case and considered it her own, when he was the one who got the first call about it and discovered the body.

He was just getting up from the table so friends and relatives could greet Brad and Donna, when his cell phone rang. He stepped out into the hall to keep his conversation private.

"Just what in the hell is going on there?" Rhonda's husband, Mark, asked as soon as Jack answered the phone. "I just saw the coverage of the funeral on TV, and they were taking Rhonda out of there on a gurney. I tried to call her cell and it went to voice mail."

Jack quickly explained the events of the morning as simply as possible. He wondered just where Mark was calling from. He hadn't been at the funeral or the visitation, so that must mean wherever he was that could be where Kitty had been taken.

"Do you think I should go to the hospital to be with her?" Mark asked. "I can be there in a couple of hours."

At least I know he's not in town. I was right, he probably had Kitty with him. I hope he's careful, from what I've heard that Kitty has claws. "Where are you?"

"I took advantage of Rhonda being on a big case and came up to my parents' cottage to do some fishing."

With the knowledge of Mark's whereabouts, Jack had a good idea where Rhonda took Kitty for safekeeping.

"I haven't had any word from the hospital, yet. When I hear something, I'll make sure someone gets in touch with you. As for Rhonda's cell, I'm sure it was still turned off because of the funeral."

By the end of the conversation, Mark seemed to have calmed down considerably. It was a good thing, too. If he was guarding Kitty, Jack didn't want her to be alone.

~ * ~

Waves of nausea and dizziness washed over Rhonda as the EMT's lifted the gurney from the back of the ambulance. Considering she'd taken a blow to her head; she knew the reaction was completely normal.

Once inside the hospital she caught a glimpse of Paul trailing along behind her. In addition, she saw several county deputies awaiting her arrival in the corridor. Considering Jack's blasé attitude at the church, the added security came as a complete surprise.

"What's going on?" she asked, once Paul joined her in the examination room.

"With all that's been happening the last few days, the media are all over this like stink on shit. It did surprise me to see the county boys here though."

Paul's mention of the media brought to mind the image that must have been splashed across the TV screens of all the major networks covering the funeral. Just the idea of such publicity sent a shiver of dread through Rhonda's body. She prayed Mark was out on the lake and Kitty found better ways to occupy her time than watching the news.

"I have to let Mark know what's going on," she said, panic sounding in her voice.

"Give me his cell number and I'll call him for you. It looks like someone is on their way in to get you treated."

Rhonda repeated Mark's cell number, just as the nurse

entered her cubical.

"I need to take your vitals," the young woman said. "After that we'll have someone from the lab come and get a blood sample."

Inwardly, Rhonda seethed. Just what did vitals and blood samples have to do with the cut on her head. Rather than voice her displeasure with having to comply with hospital regulations, she kept her mouth shut.

After a good half-hour, a doctor finally entered the room. In that time, Rhonda had seen neither hide nor hair of Paul or anyone else for that matter.

"I'm Dr. Grant," a slender young woman said as she came to Rhonda's bedside. "Let's take a look at the cut on your forehead."

"I can't believe it's as bad as everyone is making it out to be," Rhonda commented, trying to sound nonchalant.

"The EMT's did a good job in the field, but it still needs a bit of cleaning up. That will give the lidocaine a chance to work so I can get started."

The thought of getting a shot of lidocaine in her forehead made Rhonda a bit queasy, but she gritted her teeth and waited for the bite of the needle piercing her skin. To her amazement, she hardly felt the prick of the needle.

While the lidocaine numbed her skin, Rhonda could feel her eyes getting heavy. She knew the worst thing would be sleep after a head wound, but her body had a different idea.

~ * ~

Rhonda forced her eyes open. When she did, she saw Paul sitting beside the cot in the emergency room cubical.

"Good morning, Sleeping Beauty," Paul greeted her.

"I didn't mean to fall asleep. Everyone says that's not a good thing to do when you have a head injury."

"I thought the same thing, but the doctor said it was all

right. She told me to come and let her know when you wake up."

Paul started to get up to leave, but Rhonda stopped him. "Did you get in touch with Mark?"

"I did. He called Jack when he couldn't reach you on your cell. I told him once you were out of here, you'd call him and let him know you're all right."

Within moments of Paul leaving her side, Dr. Grant entered the room. "I've never had a patient fall asleep in the suture room before."

"I didn't plan on it, but I couldn't stay awake. Paul said you told him it wasn't a bad thing."

"In your case, it was just what you needed. We kept you closely monitored. It did make putting in your stitches easier. For your information, it took eight stitches to close your gash. You're lucky the scar will be covered by your hair."

Rhonda patiently allowed Dr. Grant to examine her one final time. "It looks to me as though you're ready to be released. I do want you to follow up with your personal physician in a week to get the stitches removed. Unfortunately, your uniform was soaked with blood, so we got you a set of scrubs to wear home."

Rhonda looked at the scrubs with 'Property of St. Thomas Hospital' stenciled on them. They would have to be laundered and returned, no matter how comfortable they were to wear.

"I hear you've been released," Paul said, once she was dressed in the scrubs. "Allow me to escort you back to Donna's house."

"Donna's house? Why?"

"She requested you and I stay there. It's too bad we won't be able to see them before they leave on vacation. They suggested leaving town and Jack thought it was a good idea, especially with what's been going on around them."

"I hope you know how to cook," Rhonda quipped.

"Mark does most of the cooking at our house. He gets home first, so it only makes sense."

"Give me a micro and a TV dinner and I can do wonders," Paul replied.

Rhonda laughed for the first time since this odyssey began. "We'll make a great pair. If we're lucky, Jack will have our meals catered in."

"Like that's going to happen," Paul said, joining her laughter. "Hopefully, Donna keeps a well-stocked pantry and refrigerator."

~ * ~

Although Jack argued about it, no one wanted to budge on wanting Paul and Rhonda to stay at the Kelly house.

"Look, Jack, Rhonda won't be able to return to active duty for a while," Sheriff Cantwell pointed out. "This way she can stay on the case and not get in our hair. She reminds me of a pit bull. Once she gets her teeth into something, it's almost impossible for her to let it go."

Jack knew it would do no good to argue further with the sheriff. Rhonda viewed this as her case and with good reason. She was the one who first discovered and turned in the tip on the phone messages. She also decided to stash Kitty in a safe place and declare her dead for her own protection.

He thought about the conversation he'd had with Rhonda after going back to the mansion after the fire and finding the floor safe. He knew he should have sent someone to retrieve the safe, but the events of the past two days kept him from following through with his plans.

Jack harbored no doubts about Rhonda chafing under the imposed light duty, but by being at Donna's house she could keep her hand on the pulse of things.

~ * ~

Rhonda was surprised to see Donna's car waiting for them in the parking lot of the hospital. She understood it was all part of the ruse, but she hadn't expected Jack to carry out such an extensive plan.

Once outside, Rhonda found a detailed note addressed to her on the seat of the car. After the commotion at the church, the family hadn't gone to the cemetery. Instead, they came back to the house, packed their bags, and drove toward the airport.

When they were certain no one was following them, they went to the county jail. Once there, an officer took them to a hotel room where they could make reservations for the first flight to Aruba and their unplanned impromptu getaway. A deputy then took their car to the hospital so Rhonda and Paul could use it.

Now, as they drove toward the house, Paul had a worried expression on his face.

"Something wrong?" Rhonda inquired.

"We picked up a tail at the last stop light. It looks like someone was waiting for Donna and Sean to come back from the airport. Anyone at last night's visitation or today's funeral knew Brad and Loretta planned to go back home right after this morning's service."

"I'm liking this assignment less and less. We're sitting ducks at the Kelly house if these jerks decide to firebomb it like they did the mansion? Are you sure we're being tailed?"

"Oh, yes, they're still there. Of course, the bombing is something we'll have to risk. Even though the boss doesn't want to believe it, I think you're on to something. Between him and the sheriff, they're convinced there are four wronged women behind this. You don't agree, do you?"

"Not at all. I know why they think it was women behind this, but this isn't something a woman would do.

"What about the DNA?"

"I'm not saying women weren't involved. I don't think the DNA came from sexual activity. I have a feeling it was more of a statement made after the mutilation. In other words, 'piss on you'. Besides, I doubt a woman would think of cutting off the guy's penis. That's something a guy might do to make a statement, but not a woman. Contrary to popular belief, not every woman is Lorena Bobbitt."

"So, who do you think is behind this?"

"I don't have the slightest idea, but whoever it is, they knew Karl quite well and didn't like him. I'm hoping we can find answers in the floor safe I found at the mansion after the fire."

"How did you find the floor safe? I thought the place was a total loss."

"The center part of the house was, but most of the debris ended up in the basement swimming pool. I happened to see something there and realized it was a metal box of some kind. On closer inspection, I decided it had to be a floor safe. So, I asked the chief to retrieve it for me. The problem is no one knows the combination. I asked Brad and Donna about it, and they confirmed what I already knew but they said only their dad had the combination. They also told me there is a safety deposit box at the bank. If he had any idea about the people who killed him, I'm sure it will be in either of those places, or maybe in the safe at his office downtown. From what Kitty told me he rarely threw away anything."

"Makes sense. As I recall, I've always heard he was a bit of an odd duck, and not just in the sex department."

After putting the garage door down, Paul went into the living room to watch what the people who were tailing them were doing. He returned to the garage to tell her the car went past the house without stopping, Rhonda opened the door on her side of the car. Her head ached, but she chalked it up to the injury she'd been treated for at the hospital.

Once they were in the house the phone began to ring.

Rhonda and Paul hurried into the living room to listen to the message being left by the caller.

"I took care of your cop bodyguard, Donna. Now, with your brother gone, you'll be at my mercy. I won't do anything as dramatic as I did with your old man's whore, but trust me, I will get what is due to me."

Rhonda sank into the recliner. She felt like crying after listening to the message. It certainly wasn't the emotion she expected, but with everything that had been going on lately, her nerves were on edge. If these people thought she was Donna, her life could be in danger. She'd have to be on high alert.

Chapter Nine

The night of the funeral added several more threatening calls to the list. Rhonda was glad the Kelly's had a machine like the one she installed at the mansion on Monday. In that way the chief could monitor all the calls through the phone company, taking from her shoulders the responsibility of repeating everything the callers said.

She'd talked to Mark and Kitty several times assuring them she was perfectly safe, even though she knew it was a gross understatement.

Rhonda hated being cooped up in the house with all the drapes closed and the blinds drawn. She was used to being outside rather than in the house. At least Donna had a great library with plenty of reading material in the romance genre Rhonda enjoyed.

It helped that Sean ran an Internet company out of his home, so he didn't have any reason to leave the house. The only time either of them would have to drive anywhere would be to get groceries and considering the amount of food the neighbors supplied when they heard about the murder, the cupboards, refrigerator, and freezer were all full.

Rhonda was just about to turn on the TV to break the boredom when her cell phone rang. A quick glance at the caller ID told her Jack was on the line.

"How are you doing this morning?" he questioned after exchanging the mandatory greetings.

"I have the headache from hell and not being able to open the blinds is driving me completely out of my mind. I don't know how women who don't work make it."

"Well, I've got some work you can do. I just received a

copy of the revised autopsy report. The first one was based only on the preliminary findings. I think you'll find it very interesting. The other reason I called was to see if you've been watching the national news."

"Are you kidding? I hate TV. Unfortunately, I'm so bored I was considering it. What's up?"

"Just turn it on. I'll wait."

Rhonda turned on the set then went to the station running all day news. They were talking about the fiasco on the political scene and the mass shootings going on around the country.

"What does all of this have to do with anything we're investigating?"

"Be patient."

"And now, on the national front, the home of Bradly Reedman, son of the murdered millionaire, Karl Reedman, was vandalized while he was attending his father's funeral in Wisconsin. With no one home, there were no injuries."

Rhonda stared at the TV in disbelief as the cameras focused on the front of the house where the words DEATH TO THE BASTARD'S SON were spray painted on the bricks. It was obvious the windows on the front of the house were broken out.

"I can't believe they went that far," she finally said.

"I can't believe it either, but at least Brad and Donna are safe in Aruba. I had a call from them this morning after they heard about the vandalism."

Rhonda breathed a sigh of relief. Even though she and the Reedman's didn't run in the same social circles, she'd come to genuinely like both Brad and Donna.

"Another thing I wanted to ask you about," Jack said, interrupting her thoughts. "Did you see Susan Barclay at either the visitation or the funeral?"

Rhonda wracked her brain. With so much going on, she hadn't given Susan much thought. The only reference to the woman was Kitty saying her friend needed to grieve privately. Since Rhonda hadn't been concerned with Susan or her whereabouts, she'd almost forgotten about her. Although originally Rhonda had been assigned to guard Kitty and Susan, the latter's disappearance, along with Kitty's explanation removed that responsibility from her shoulders.

"As far as I can remember, she wasn't at either of them. Are you trying to contact her?"

"I have been, but I'm hitting a brick wall. Her office says she's cancelled all her appointments for the next two weeks. I haven't been able to get an answer at either her apartment or her cell. It looks like she dropped off the face of the earth. With the investigation going on, it doesn't look good for her."

"Have you sent anyone to her apartment to check on her?"

"The county is sending someone over there this morning. I'll keep you posted on what they find."

Leaving the TV on, Rhonda went down to the lower level of the house to talk with Paul. She figured she'd find him either in Sean's office or the elaborate fitness center adjacent to it. Wealth did have its perks.

She found Paul in the office, staring intently at the computer screen. As she peered over his shoulder, she could read the online version of the story concerning the vandalism of Brad's home.

"I just had a call from the chief about this story. I can't believe these people would go clear out to Denver."

"I can. Whoever is behind this wants the entire family dead. From the calls we've been getting here, it seems to be very clear."

"I'm sure it does. The chief also got the autopsy information back. He's emailing it to us so we can look it over."

"Since he called you, why don't you check your account

first?"

Rhonda was relieved to see the email from the chief in her inbox, along with the paperclip symbol indicating an attachment was also there.

Once the document filled the screen, she printed off two copies so she and Paul could read it at the same time.

"Look at this," Paul said, pointing to the line that gave cause of death.

Either he was a faster reader than she or he didn't get bogged down with all the medical jargon.

Rhonda scanned her copy until she found the place Paul indicated.

The victim was injected with a paralytic drug to keep him conscious but unable to fight off his attackers. His penis was amputated while he was still alive, but he suffered a fatal heart attack before he was shot.

"Well, that certainly blows a hole in Sheriff Cantwell's theory," Rhonda said. "I'm sure he figured it was one of the gunshots that did the dirty deed. The way this report reads, shooting him was more of an afterthought."

"It looks like more a statement to me," Paul added. "As for the DNA, it's like you thought. It came from urine and not vaginal secretions. The interesting thing is that two of the females are close relatives to the victim."

Rhonda's mind immediately jumped to Donna. Since Karl had been an only child, there were no siblings to put into the mix and his parents died twenty years earlier. Donna was the only choice, but who could the second woman be?

"Do you think the DNA of one of the close relatives could have come from Donna?"

"Not from the phone calls we've been getting. Besides, the chief told me they had Brad and Donna take DNA tests. Further down, this report rules her out. It's possible with the number of affairs this guy had, he has more than one daughter running around out there."

"As well as a son or two. That sheds a whole new light on things. The problem is most of his affairs were with married women. If one got pregnant by him, it's entirely possible she let her husband believe the kid was his."

"It's entirely possible they could have blackmailed Reedman. If that were the case, the money would have stopped coming when the kid reached the age of eighteen. If that is the case, the gene pool is endless."

Rhonda's mind spun with the possibilities. A man with Karl's wealth would hardly miss the money spent to support the children conceived during his extra marital affairs. The problem would be finding who got the payments. It was entirely possible they would have been made with cash without leaving any kind of paper trail.

The breaking of glass upstairs shattered Rhonda's mental ramblings. Running up the stairs, she saw a large rock lying on the living room floor at the same time she heard the phone begin to ring then take a message from the caller.

"How do you like our newest message, Bitch?"

Rhonda returned her gaze to the rock with a paper attached with masking tape. "What is it with this guy and rocks? Where does he think he is, Bedrock? We certainly aren't the Flintstones here."

Paul's footsteps from behind her were the first indication he'd followed her up the stairs.

"Don't touch it," he cautioned. "I know you can't get prints from the rock, but you could from the paper and the tape. Besides, there could be DNA on it. We don't want to get it mixed up with yours."

Rhonda turned and noticed Paul put on a pair of latex gloves. She watched as he removed the note from the rock lying in a bed of shattered glass from the plate glass window.

"It seems our tormentor is a poet. Listen to this:
Rocks are for throwing
When I get mad

The money you're inheriting
Is what we should have had,"

"One thing is for certain, he's no Carl Sandburg, but it does give credence to your theory. Now we just need to find out the identities of Karl's other kids."

Before Paul could reply, Rhonda's cell phone rang.

"This is Jack," came from the other end as soon as she connected to the call. "I got a call from the county and they asked me to come over to Susan Barclay's apartment."

"Is she there?" Rhonda asked, envisioning them finding her dead for several days and stinking to high heaven.

"No, the place is completely cleaned out. Something tells me she decided to get out of town fast. Maybe it was the attempt on Kitty's life that sent her packing."

"As far as she's concerned, Kitty is dead. She might think she could be next, although I doubt, he would leave money for his mistress."

"That's a possibility. It's something we must work on. In the meantime, how are things going with you?"

"Oh, they're just ducky. Someone just threw a rock through the living room window with a note attached to it. Just after it landed, we got another call. If I were Donna, I wouldn't feel exactly safe here."

"Since this guy thinks you're Donna, you need to get out of there. I'm on my way and I'll bring the county boys with me. In the meantime, I want you and Paul always armed. It's hard telling what this guy will do next."

Sirens screamed in the quiet neighborhood where Donna and Sean's house sat. Since Rhonda had just gotten off the phone, she wondered if one of the neighbors had called 911.

Turning, she saw Paul standing in the doorway leading to the kitchen. "I called them while you were talking to Jack."

He motioned her to come into the kitchen and for the first time, she realized anyone could have broken the kitchen window and come to get them. With the exception of Mark, she'd never had anyone to take the burden of responsibility from her shoulders. Rhonda's father died when she was in junior high school. After the funeral her mother worked two jobs to make ends meet, leaving Rhonda to take care of herself and make many of the decisions when it came to running the household. Having made so many meals as a teenager, it was no wonder she allowed Mark to dominate her kitchen. Having been self-sufficient when she was younger, served her well. No one questioned her decision to attend the police academy at the local technical college.

Paul opened the garage door to allow the officers entry into the house. She knew he did it to not disturb the crime scene in the living room. Thankfully, Paul used gloves so as not to leave prints that would confuse the investigation.

"Did you see who threw the rock?" Steve, the officer who spent the night there the night before the funeral, asked.

"We were both in the downstairs office. We heard the glass breaking and found the rock as well as the note."

Rhonda watched as Paul handed Steve a Ziploc bag from the kitchen with the note in it. It wasn't a regulation evidence bag, but Paul made do by searching Donna's kitchen for a suitable replacement.

"Either this guy is taking delight in tormenting us, or he's not playing with a full deck. Who throws rocks anymore?"

From the corner of her eye, Rhonda saw Jack pull up in front of the house. Without listening to the discussion further, she stepped into the kitchen and pushed the button to open the garage door. Even with the broken window, she knew Paul closed it for security reasons.

"Did you get a chance to read the autopsy report?" Jack asked, as he entered the kitchen.

She thought the question was redundant, since they'd talked moments earlier. She tried to remember if they'd discussed the autopsy report and decided they hadn't.

"We were reading it when all hell broke loose up here."

She motioned toward the shattered living room window.

"Like I said earlier, you can't continue to stay here," Jack said, the concern in his voice genuine.

"I don't see why not. Donna and Sean would stay here. This is their home. We'll have to get someone to board up the window and once that's done, we'll be perfectly safe."

"Perfectly safe, my ass. What if they try firebombing this place like they did out at the mansion?"

"For one thing, there are too many neighbors. At the mansion, it was a secluded location. They never expected someone to call it in so quickly. At the time, there was the element of surprise in their favor, or so they thought. That said, they wanted the place to burn to the ground."

"You're right there. It looks like they cut the phone lines after making the last call. Of course, we're off track. What did you make of the autopsy report."

Rhonda wondered if this was the time for her to voice her opinion on the case. Throwing caution to the wind, she took a deep breath before she began.

"You know, I've listened to all the messages. They all seem to point in the same direction. With all of Karl's affairs, it's entirely possible he had several children out there. He doesn't seem to be the type to want to use a condom. If he'd been supporting them in the past, it's only logical they would want a piece of the inheritance and didn't want to wait for him to die naturally."

Jack frowned. "Makes sense, but how did they find each other? I mean people don't go around saying, 'I'm Karl Reedman's bastard, how about you?' Besides, why go after Donna and Brad? It takes a lot of balls to want to kill your own brother and sister."

"I haven't figured out how they found each other, but I think they've gotten greedy and want all the pie rather than just part of it. What clinched it for me was some of the female DNA came from close relatives. The only close relative Karl had is Donna and she's been ruled out."

"It's a nice theory, but one that's too hard to confirm. For now, I'm more concerned with Susan Barclay's whereabouts."

Rhonda tried to hide her disappointment over the way Jack put aside her theory. She wondered if the suggestion would have carried more weight coming from Paul rather than her.

"Have you been able to open the floor safe?" she asked, changing the subject.

"Not yet. The county boys don't think we'll find much there. They're more concerned about what Karl might have kept in the lock boxes. We've checked the local banks with no luck. It seems Karl pulled all his accounts about four years ago."

"That doesn't surprise me. I heard some scuttlebutt about how he wanted to borrow some money for a new project and all three of the banks here turned him down. It's possible he had more money on paper than in actuality. With his cash flow tied up in investments, I can't blame the smaller banks for turning him down."

At least on this point, she decided Jack must agree with her. It was evident he'd tired of the conversation, since he drifted off toward the living room to confer with the officer investigating the rock throwing incident.

Tired of her male counterparts treating her like the invisible woman, Rhonda made her way toward the bedrooms. She'd given little thought to the notes she made at the visitation until now.

Rhonda prayed Brad and Donna sent the visitation and funeral guest book back to the house. Without hesitation, she walked into the master bedroom in the hope she'd find what she was looking for.

After an extensive search of the room, she decided to look elsewhere. Her next room would be the office. *This probably should have been the first place I decided to look.*

"Where did you get off to?" Jack asked, when Rhonda walked back into the kitchen.

"I was looking for something in the master bedroom. I figured you had Paul to fill you in and you didn't need me."

She knew her tone sounded bitchy, but she didn't care. To Jack and the other men, she was little more than window dressing or maybe just a pain in the ass.

"You should have been with us," Jack said sarcastically. "You're a vital part of this investigation. What, exactly, were you looking for anyway?"

The words, *like hell I am*, formed on her tongue, but she bit back the nasty retort. "I was trying to find the visitation and funeral sign-in book. Remember I told you about those two couples who didn't quite belong?"

She waited while Jack checked his memory. From the expression on his face, she knew he didn't have the slightest idea what she was talking about, even though he nodded his head in agreement.

"I thought maybe I could get a name to start investigating."

Jack rolled his eyes. "I'll check with the funeral director. It could still be with him. In the meantime, if you find it, let me know."

His condescending tone grated on Rhonda's nerves. Thank goodness she'd long ago learned to mask her true emotions. With her head aching from her injury, she was finding it harder and harder to blow off Jack's male chauvinistic attitude.

Chapter Ten

Jack looked at the charred floor safe now resting in the back seat of his car. When Rhonda asked him about it, he didn't want to let on he hadn't sent someone out to retrieve it.

From the recesses of his mind, he recalled Paul saying he was good at deciphering combinations. At least having the safe at the Kelly house would give the two of them something to occupy their time.

The drive across town was uneventful. He didn't expect anything different after the rock throwing incident this morning.

The streets of the subdivision were literally deserted. With everything that transpired in the past week, it was no wonder. After such a brutal murder, arson, and all the threats, he didn't blame parents for keeping their kids inside.

The boarded-up picture window of the Kelly house made it look more like a scene of a natural disaster than one of the most upscale neighborhoods in town.

Earlier, Paul gave him a garage door opener so he could pull into the garage rather than park in front of the house. Considering the deserted street stretching before and behind him posed no threat, he thought the precaution was an overreaction, but he'd humor his officer.

Pushing the button, Jack pulled into the empty spot in the three-car garage. Once he cleared the door, he again hit the button to close everything up tight.

Before entering the house, he called out a greeting. Stepping into the kitchen he heard the phone ring. The message was just starting when he walked further into the house.

"How convenient for the cops to have their own garage door opener. It's a shame I don't have one."

The voice was familiar to Jack and sent chills down his spine.

"H-How close do you think this guy is?" Jack asked when he entered the living room.

Rhonda looked up from sweeping the glass from the hardwood floor. "It's hard telling where these creeps are. The important thing is they seem to know everything we do. It's a complete mystery to me. Let me guess, there wasn't a car in sight when you pulled up, right?"

Jack nodded. He hated it when she was right. "The reason I came over is that damnable floor safe. No one seems to be able to get it open. After I left here, I remembered Paul saying he was good at getting into combination safes."

He intentionally left out the part about not retrieving it until today. There was no need to add fuel to the fire already raging in Rhonda's mind.

"Where is it?" Paul asked, as he entered the room.

"It's sitting on a tarp in the back of my car. I certainly didn't want to get my seat all dirty from the damn thing."

He watched as Rhonda put down her broom and dustpan to follow them out to the garage. Considering he'd managed to get the damn thing into his car, just about putting out his back, he welcomed Paul's help in getting it out.

Rhonda was quick to open a door at the back of the garage. Beyond it was one of the best-equipped workshops Jack ever saw.

"I'd like to stick around and see what you come up with but duty calls. With the two of you here, we're running short handed."

~ * ~

"That son of a bitch," Rhonda complained once she saw

84

the garage door go down. "I can tell by looking at this thing, no one has touched it since the fire."

Paul scrutinized the lock. "No one has tried to open it, that's for sure. I'm willing to bet he went out to the fire scene to get it this morning because he forgot all about it."

Rhonda watched mesmerized while Paul listened to the click of the tumblers in order to figure out the combination.

"Were you a safe cracker in a former life?" she teased when the door to the safe opened.

"Hardly. My dad was a locksmith. I worked for him in high school and learned how to open combination locks. He told me I was a natural, since he always had trouble with those things. It was my grandfather who taught me to do this. He said he was getting too old to keep working and to train someone to take his place in the business. Of course, I went into law enforcement. My brother stayed on and was able to take Grandpa's place when he retired last year."

Rhonda marveled at how little she knew about her co-worker. As she watched the door of the safe open, she felt a bit the same as she did as a kid on Christmas morning waiting to see what Santa brought her.

"I think Jack is right. There are only some envelopes in here," Paul said, disappointment sounding in his voice.

Nevertheless, he pulled out a handful of envelopes from the safe and gave them to Rhonda.

"Well, I'll be damned," he commented as he looked further into the interior of the safe. "This might be interesting."

Rhonda watched as he took a book that could be a daily journal from the box. Rather than opening anything in the workshop, they took the contents of the safe into the kitchen so they could sit at the table and examine the contents.

"This was your find," Paul said. "You should be the first one to see what it contains."

Rhonda could feel herself blush at his compliment. "I wouldn't call it 'my' find."

"Of course, it is. With everything that's going on lately no one thought of poking around in the debris at the mansion. If you hadn't seen the safe, I doubt it would have been discovered."

Rhonda knew he was right. It wouldn't be long before the bulldozers would be coming in to clear up the mess left by the fire, to say nothing of the water the fire department used to keep it contained just to the central area of the house.

Instead of looking for a letter opener, Rhonda pulled a paring knife from the knife block on the counter closest to the table.

"Oh, my god," she exclaimed when she took the contents from the first envelope.

"Is that what it looks like?" Paul asked, crossing the room to look over her shoulder.

"It sure is. There are twenty one-hundred dollar bills in here," she replied, after taking the time to count the money. "This has to be his emergency stash."

She stopped herself from saying the money would come in handy for Kitty. Since very few people in town, other than Jack and Sheriff Cantwell knew Kitty didn't die in the fire, she certainly didn't want to let the cat out of the bag at this point.

After opening the second envelope, she pulled out several sheets of paper, each with an envelope attached. "These look like death threats to me," she observed before handing them to Paul. "There's no return address but they were all mailed from Madison."

"Which doesn't mean diddly. The only saving grace is the envelope flaps are still intact. At least we could conceivably get a DNA sample from them. If we're lucky, one of them could match the ones left by those close female relatives who pee on him at the crime scene."

Paul produced another makeshift evidence bag and slid the incriminating letters inside. Even though Rhonda briefly scanned them, she wished she took the time to read them in their entirety.

The next envelope contained the signed prenuptial agreements from wives two, three and four. "It looks like he covered his bases where his ex-wives were concerned. There's even the divorce decree from his first marriage at the bottom of the stack. It looks like she took him for quite a financial ride. I don't have to guess his reason for asking the others to sign a prenup."

The final envelope contained insurance papers as well as a revised will dated three days before Karl's death. Reading over the will, Rhonda saw bequeaths to several charities, but the bulk of the estate was to be divided equally between Brad and Donna.

"I don't see any surprises here."

She reached for the journal. Opening the first page, she saw it began on January first. Apparently, he was in the habit of making notes on his everyday activities. If that were the case, they'd have to find the ones dating back over the past thirty years. If he kept them, it was entirely possible he stored them either in a safe deposit box at whatever bank he had been using that year or put them in a larger safe at the office in town.

Taking the journal, she went into the living room to sit in the recliner. The entries were pretty much run of the mill until she read the one dated January twentieth.

"Listen to this entry," she called to Paul.

She waited until he came from the kitchen before, she began to read the entry aloud.

"Bitter cold today. Can't understand these kids. Sure, I fathered them, but their mothers were well-compensated. I owe them nothing and yet they think I should support them for the rest of their lives. Even Brad and Donna don't expect that. They should get down on their knees and kiss my feet for giving them life."

"Conceited son of a bitch," Paul said after hearing the passage. "At least he acknowledged them, even if they weren't legal."

"It's possible this is when the first contact by them as adults started. It's funny, since the first threesome with Susan happened on the seventh of January. Is it a coincidence or something else?"

Rhonda knew her question was one without an answer. Only time would tell who the guilty parties were.

"I think we need to find the rest of the journals. At least we might find out which of his affairs produced children. Why don't you get out of here for a while and go down to his office. Maybe you can see what you can find in his safe at that location."

Paul agreed with her. Once he left, Rhonda continued reading the documented details of Karl's private life. The man had a tendence to ramble on and on about his sex life, including his evenings spent with both Kitty and Susan as well as the women he had affairs with during the first three months of the year.

Before she could read past the first of April, the words started to blur together. Vowing only to rest her eyes for a moment, she was soon sound asleep.

Rhonda woke with a start. Had she dreamed someone was jiggling the doorknob for the front door? The noise came again, making her glad the deadbolt was in place. With the front window boarded up and the front door made of solid steel, she had no chance to see who was trying to get in. It would have helped if the door had a peephole, but apparently, Sean and Donna saw no need of it.

Drawing her gun, she placed a call to dispatch for backup. Even if the unthinkable happened and someone did get into the house, she'd have the drop on them, and backup would arrive quickly.

For the first time she realized Sean and Donna turned this house into a mini-Fort Knox. Unlike most of the upscale houses in the neighborhood, there were no patio doors. Only the picture window was vulnerable, since the other windows, except for the small garden window over the kitchen sink, sported heavy grillwork.

Again, she heard the rattling at the door. In order to be ready for the intruder to break in, she stepped into the hallway with her gun drawn, taking a shooting stance.

From down the block, she heard the sirens and wished she'd asked them to come quietly, At the same moment, the rattling stopped. It was entirely possible whoever was trying to gain entrance heard the sirens in time to make good in his escape.

Within seconds, she heard the garage door open, signaling either Paul or Jack had also arrived. Had they heard the dispatch call or was their arrival merely a coincidence?

"Stop, police."

Rhonda heard the shout even through the closed door. It was followed by the report of a pistol.

"Are you okay?"

Paul's question startled her, even though she expected him to be in the house. She turned; her revolver trained on anyone who could possibly be an intruder.

"It's me, Rhonda. Everything is under control," he said.

She focused on his face and saw the fear in his eyes. She could have easily shot him, thinking only of the person who tried to break into the house. Obediently, she lowered her gun.

"S-someone was trying to break in."

"I know, I followed the squad cars here. I came on in since I figured they had things under control, and I wanted to make certain you were alright. For now, let's get you into a comfortable chair. You're shaking like a leaf."

Rhonda allowed Paul to pry the gun from her hand and lead her back to the recliner where she'd been sleeping earlier.

"I-I was sleeping when the sound of someone trying to break in woke me. If I'd been more alert, I would have asked for a silent response. Maybe then, we might have caught them in the act."

Tears were rolling down her cheeks as she lamented what she saw as a dereliction of duty.

"No one can fault you for falling asleep. If anyone is to blame, it's me. I shouldn't have left you here alone. It's entirely possible they saw me leave and thought no one was at home. If that is the case, it's a good thing you were here to call dispatch."

The phone rang just as a deputy entered the house through the open garage door. Rhonda made eye contact with him, to make certain he didn't answer the ringing phone.

"It's a shame the cops got here when they did. I had quite a surprise for you. Oh well, it's your loss. I was lucky, those cops came with their sirens blaring, giving me a heads-up to get the hell out of Dodge. Oh, by the way, those guys certainly can't claim to be sharpshooters. They couldn't hit the broad side of a barn."

The deputy looked skeptical. "I don't know what he's talking about. We winged one of the suspects and my partner has him in custody. Your caller could have been the second one who got away."

~ * ~

Jack followed the ambulance as it turned into the subdivision where the Kelly home sat. If something happened to Rhonda because Paul left her alone, he'd rip that boy a new one before he fired his ass.

As soon as his car stopped, he jumped out and ran to the ambulance.

"What happened here?" he asked the officer standing beside the open back door of the ambulance.

As he got closer, he recognized Steve from the funeral.

"Rhonda called into dispatch and said someone was trying to break into the house. By the time we got here, two suspects were running down the street. We called for them to stop and when they didn't, we fired. We got one of them but the other one got away."

Jack breathed a sigh of relief that Rhonda wasn't the victim being rolled toward the ambulance on a gurney. When he saw the kid, he recognized him as fifteen-year-old Aaron Miller.

"What's going on Aaron?" Jack asked.

"They shot me. Just like that they shot me."

Jack realized he'd have to go carefully with the boy. He had Down's Syndrome and wouldn't understand exactly what they were talking about. His parents made certain he led a relatively sheltered life.

"What were you doing here?"

Aaron looked up with tears in his eyes. "Mr. Kelly said he got locked out of his house. He asked me to help him get in."

"Do you know Mr. Kelly, Aaron?"

"I know he lives here, but I've never seen him up close before. Did I do something wrong?"

"No, Aaron, you were just trying to help. We'll get you to the hospital and call your mother."

"We're going to press charges against the boy," Steve said. "He had to know the guy wasn't Sean Kelly."

"If it was anyone else, I'd agree with you, but not Aaron. You can tell he has a problem just by looking at him. He's no more capable of being part of a murder plot than I am."

"How do I know you aren't capable of murder? Hell, we're all capable of unthinkable things. Given his mental state, he could have been talked into anything. As for his capacity, he knows who you are. He can't be that slow."

"Of course, he knew me. I've helped him cross the street to go to school ever since he was in kindergarten. Even though he should be in high school, he takes special ed classes at the elementary school."

"That's enough, Chief," Steve said, stepping between Jack and the gurney. "The boy is a suspect. I need to read him his rights."

"Look, that can wait until his mother is present. I'll have her meet you at the hospital."

Steve waited until Aaron was loaded into the ambulance before replying. "In case you've forgotten, this is a murder case. That said, this kid is the first solid lead we've had so butt out."

Without further comment, Steve climbed into the front seat of the ambulance before it pulled away.

Jack fumed but decided not to argue further. Instead, he called the station to have Melanie get in touch with Phyllis Miller so she could be at the hospital before Steve read Aaron his rights.

Once inside the garage, Jack hit the button to close the door and make the house secure. Entering through the kitchen he could hear voices coming from the living room. Following the sound he saw Rhonda, Paul and a deputy engaged in conversation.

"Deputy Newman told us they have a suspect in custody," Rhonda said, excitement sounding in her voice.

"They have Aaron Miller in custody. The poor kid thought he was helping Mr. Kelly get back into his house."

"Aaron can't possibly have anything to do with this," Paul declared. "His mentality level can't be much more than eight or nine years old."

"It doesn't matter," Deputy Newman said. "He was running with the other man who was trying to break in here. With all the threats, this kid could be an accomplice and he could be charged with murder and arson."

Jack seethed with anger. Several years ago, Aaron was caught shoplifting candy down at Murphy's store, but nothing ever came from it. Everyone in town knew Aaron didn't have the mental capacity to know right from wrong.

Deputy Newman left the house and went back out to his squad car, leaving Jack to question the actions of the county sheriff's office. Aaron was no more involved in this mess than the man in the moon.

~ * ~

Rhonda wished she could be at the hospital when Phyllis Miller arrived. They'd been friends for years. She knew Aaron's arrest would hit his mother hard. Phyllis had been a single mother for the past ten years, since her husband Nick, had been killed in an ATV accident. It certainly hadn't been easy for Phyllis but up until now, she'd been coping.

"I can't believe Aaron had anything to do with this," Rhonda commented. "He's such a sweet kid. I doubt he even knows about the murder. He seems to be in his own little world most of the time."

"I couldn't agree more," Jack replied. "Aaron told me this man said he was Sean Kelly and he needed help getting into his house, since he locked himself out."

"Knowing Aaron," Phil added, "I can see him wanting to help someone in trouble."

"I want to go down to the hospital," Rhonda said. "Phyllis will need a friend there with her."

"I don't think that's such a good idea," Paul cautioned. "You're exhausted, Rhonda. Add that to the fact you're still recovering from your own trip to the emergency room, and I think you should rest."

"That doesn't matter. Right now, I'm a cop. Phyllis is my friend, and she needs any support she can get. It hasn't been easy for her raising Aaron alone. If he ends up being

93

charged with murder and arson when all he wanted to do was to help someone out, it will be a miscarriage of justice."

"Look Rhonda, I can see both sides of this," Jack declared. "I do think you need to be there in your capacity as a police officer. Someone needs to look out for Aaron's interests and who better than you? As a friend of the family, you know what Aaron's mental status is. I think you could do some good with the county boys. As for going to the hospital, the wound wasn't that serious. Until we know where they have him, it's best if you stay here where you're relatively safe."

Rhonda's phone rang before she could protest. She checked the caller ID and saw the number she knew belonged to Phyllis Miller.

"Oh, Rhonda, they've arrested Aaron. He didn't have anything to do with the murders and he's in custody. They're taking him to jail. He's scared to death. Can you come down to the jail to be with us? He trusts you."

Before answering her friend, she took a deep breath. "I'm with chief Franks. I'll have him bring me down, right away."

"I don't like this one little bit," Paul declared. "We know what these people can do. They've firebombed the Reedman mansion. They've killed not only Karl, but also Kitty Reedman. They've played David and Goliath with Rhonda at the funeral, and today they broke the window before trying to break in. What's to say they won't try to do something more to Rhonda once she leaves here."

"It's a chance I'm willing to take. I can't let anyone railroad Aaron for something he had no part in. I'm going down to the jail and I don't want to hear another word about it."

"Are you going to let her go?" Paul asked.

"Have you ever tried to tangle with a wildcat? That's what it's like to go against Rhonda when she has her mind set on something. Sheriff Cantwell called her a 'pit bull'. As far as I'm concerned, I'm content that calling her a pit bull is a misnomer. She's a hell of a lot prettier than any damn pit bull I've ever seen, but she's just as tenacious."

"Thanks for the compliment, I think." Rhonda winked at Jack. "I'll be ready to go down to the jail with you in just a minute. While I'm gone, maybe you can look for that funeral guest book."

"Rhonda's right," Jack agreed. "I called the funeral home, and they sent it with Brad and Donna when they left the church yesterday. They must have sent all the flowers here as well, since this place looks like an extension of the floral shop downtown. I'll keep an eye on Rhonda, so you don't have to worry about her. I'll also ask the county to send someone over to be with you."

Rhonda smiled at her small victory, as she went to the bathroom to splash some water on her face and put on a little lipstick. If she were going down to the county jail, she wanted to look presentable. She wouldn't be in uniform, but that would be for the best. Aaron knew her as his friend, not one of the officers who shot and arrested him. Who now were holding him for something he knew nothing about.

Chapter Eleven

Rhonda knew her jeans and sweatshirt didn't make her look like one of the officers who came and went from the county jail on a regular basis. She prayed she'd be able to see Aaron and put his mind at ease. This couldn't be easy for him to understand.

"Oh, Rhonda, I knew you'd be here. I haven't been able to see Aaron."

Phyllis threw her arms around Rhonda's neck and began to cry bitterly.

"That's not right. Aaron is a minor. They have no right to keep you from being with him. Have you contacted a lawyer yet?"

Phyllis nodded. "I called Seth Fisher. He's in court but his secretary said his partner would be here within the hour. I don't know anything about the partner. Seth was the one who handled things when my husband was killed."

Rhonda thought for a moment. "From what I hear, his partner is well-versed in criminal law. His name is Calvin Wentworth. It's said he's good at what he does. In my book he'd be far better than Seth."

Phyllis looked relieved. "Can you see if they'll let me be with my son. He must be scared half to death."

"We'll see what we can do, won't we, Jack?"

He looked at her not as her boss, her superior, but as an equal.

"I'll see what I can do. It's not right for Phyllis not to be in there with him."

It took about ten minutes for one of the deputies to take Rhonda to the interrogation room where Aaron sat by himself.

At first glance, Rhonda felt her stomach churn. The boy looked pale, as though the loss of blood drained away his color. His left arm rested in a sling. She hadn't known the extent of his injuries, but it was evident just where he'd been wounded. His right arm was shackled to the chair as though he were a common criminal.

"What did I do wrong, Rhonda?" Aaron asked, his voice sounding as though he would burst into tears at any moment.

"You didn't do anything wrong, but the officers don't know you the same way we do."

"I want my mom. They won't let me see her."

"I know you do. She is here and is waiting for someone else to come before she can be with you."

"I want to see her now. I don't understand what's going on."

Tears rolled down Aaron's cheeks, breaking Rhonda's heart. Before she could calm his fears, a deputy entered the room. He motioned for her to join him on the other side of the room out of earshot from Aaron.

"Chief Franks tells me you know this young man, Officers Pohs. Do you think you can explain things to him?" His voice was hardly louder than a whisper.

"I can do that, but I want to wait until his lawyer gets here. For now, I just want to make him feel more comfortable. He's a minor, and I don't know why you haven't allowed his mother to be here with him."

"You know this is a murder investigation and…"

"…and nothing," Rhonda interrupted. "We've told everyone who would listen he's not involved in any of this. Why is it you don't believe us?"

"Let's see, first he was trying to break into the house where there has been a lot of threats made. Secondly, he refuses to name the man he was with at the time."

"Did it ever occur to you that he doesn't know who the man is? From what I hear, the man told him he was Sean Kelly.

Aaron thought he was helping a neighbor."

"If he were a neighbor, wouldn't the boy have recognized him?"

Rhonda shook her head in disbelief of what the deputy was saying. "In case you haven't noticed, Aaron has a problem. He recognizes me because I live next door to him and see him on a regular basis. Our neighborhood is several blocks away from where the Kelly's live. Before you ask, let me explain. One of the things Aaron enjoys doing is riding his bike. I doubt there is anyone in town who doesn't know who he is. He's such a sweet kid, everyone looks out for him."

The door to the interrogation room opened and a well-dressed man entered, along with Phyllis Miller.

"I'm Calvin Wentworth. I represent Aaron."

He shook hands with both the deputy and Rhonda.

"We need to ask Aaron a few questions," the deputy declared.

"I'm here to look out for his interests, and if there's anything I don't think he should answer, I'll intervene."

The deputy sat across from Aaron and started asking questions. The only response was Aaron's sobs.

"Can I try?" Rhonda asked. "Since he knows me, he might be more responsive."

The deputy nodded and got up from the chair, indicating Rhonda should take his place.

"Aaron," Rhonda began. "You know I would never hurt you."

Aaron sniffed loudly. With his right hand shackled, he was unable to wipe the tears from his eyes.

"I know you wouldn't."

"That's good. The man who asked you to help him was a very bad man. He wanted to hurt Mr. and Mrs. Kelly. Can you tell me what happened?"

Aaron looked up at Mr. Wentworth. When the man nodded, he returned his attention to Rhonda.

"I was riding my bike and he stopped me. He said he lived a couple of blocks over and he needed help getting into his house. I asked him why he needed help and he said he went out to do some yard work and forgot his keys. He told me the door locked behind him and his wife was away from home. I wanted to help him."

"Of course, you did, Aaron. Do you know Mr. Kelly?"

"I've heard his name and know he lived in the big house where the man took me."

"Can you tell me what the man looked like?"

Aaron looked at her as though he was trying to visualize the man and put into words what he was seeing.

"I-I can't explain it."

Rhonda thought for a moment, before she asked her next question. All his life, Aaron had been a very talented artist. It was almost miraculous that he'd been compensated for his disability by being given a very special gift.

"Could you draw me a picture of what the man looked like?"

Arron's face brightened. "I like to draw pictures, Rhonda. I can draw you a picture, I know I can."

She turned her attention to the deputy and Aaron's lawyer. The deputy looked skeptical, but Calvin nodded his agreement.

"I've heard about the young man's talent. I think it would be best if you could bring him in some paper and colored pencils."

Once the deputy left the room, Phyllis hurried to her son's side. Carefully she embraced him.

"Why did the policeman shoot me, Mom? You always told me they were there to protect me if I was in any trouble."

Phyllis looked to Rhonda for an answer to her son's question.

"Did they tell you to stop?"

Aaron nodded.

"Did you stop?"

"N-no. I was scared. I just wanted to go home."

"That's why they shot. They didn't know who you were and the man who asked you to help him is a bad man. He's been threatening to do some not nice things to the Kelly's."

"Mrs. Kelly's daddy was killed. Did the man do it?" Aaron asked, his eyes wide with what could be called fear. With Aaron it was sometimes hard to tell.

Rhonda marveled at the fact Aaron even knew about the murder. "It's possible. That's why we need your help to tell us what the man looked like. We don't know who we're looking for."

"Would I be a hero like the ones on Saturday morning cartoons?"

"In my book you would, but we have to convince the deputies you were just trying to be a good citizen."

The deputy returned to the room with another man. "This is Deputy Preston," the first deputy said. "He's our sketch artist. He wanted to be here to see what Aaron can give us."

"Is it all right if I sit in and watch you draw?" Deputy Preston asked Aaron. "I like to draw, too. I enjoy watching someone who is as good as they tell me you are."

Rhonda silently applauded Deputy Preston for knowing how to put Aaron at ease. After Aaron's right hand was unshackled, he took the pencils and began to draw a picture of the man who asked him for help. Since his left hand was in the sling, he couldn't hold the paper, so Deputy Preston helped him with that aspect of the art of drawing the picture.

It took almost two hours for Aaron to finish the picture that would incriminate the man who asked him for help.

Rhonda always knew his art was good, but she never knew the amount of detail he could put in his work. Slowly, the features of a man in his early twenties began to appear on the paper. The picture even included a mole on the man's cheek, To Rhonda's surprise, the man carried a solid resemblance to Donna. It certainly confirmed her speculations about the people behind not only the murder but also the arson.

"I think you have quite a career in store for you Aaron," Deputy Preston declared. "You're a very talented artist. This picture will help the police more than anything else we've had so far in this case."

"Is he free to go?" Phyllis asked, her voice laced with skepticism.

Before anyone in the room could answer, Sheriff Cantwell and Chief Franks joined them.

"We've been discussing this," Sheriff Cantwell said. "From everything I've heard I think Aaron was in the wrong place at the wrong time and he got scared. I don't blame him. I'd be scared too."

"As far as we're concerned," Jack added, "Aaron is a hero. When the people behind this are finally arrested, it will be because of the work he's done here today."

Chapter Twelve

Rhonda waited until Aaron was released, with the apologies of the sheriff's office, to his mother's custody. From the hushed conversation between Phyllis and Calvin, Rhonda got the impression a lawsuit would be filed.

"You did a great job with Aaron in there," Jack said.

His compliment came as a complete surprise to Rhonda.

"Thank you, Chief. I'm certain you would have done the same thing. Fortunately, I've known Aaron all his life and living next door to him gives me a lot of insight into his personality."

"You make it sound easy. I'm afraid I haven't been giving you enough credit for what you do."

Of course, you don't, Rhonda wanted to scream. Instead, she held her tongue. It was best she took the compliment in silence than make a big deal out of it.

"Before we go back to the Kelly house, I want to stop at my place and pick up some clean clothes."

"That reminds me, I called the funeral director again about the guest book. He said with all the confusion the day of the funeral, he forgot to send it over to the house with the flowers. I wish he had told me that the first time I talked to him. It would have saved Paul a lot of time looking for it. I'll drop you off at your place and you can go over and pick it up. That way, you can take your time in packing what you need."

The fact Jack remembered the book at all impressed Rhonda. Once inside her house, she turned her cell phone on. She no more than activated it when it began to ring.

"What's going on?" Mark's worried voice greeted her. "I've been calling you since early this morning. I told Kitty if

I didn't get an answer this time, I'd be driving down there."

"It's been a busy day," she replied.

"The news says there was an arrest. Was it anyone we know?"

Rhonda wondered how she was going to explain to Mark it was Aaron the sheriff's office arrested.

"It's a long story. The arrest turned out to be in error. They arrested Aaron Miller…"

"Aaron?" Mark exclaimed, interrupting her.

"Calm down," she cautioned, before going on to explain the turn of events the case took this morning. "Jack and I went down to the jail. They allowed me to question Aaron. A man asked him to help him get into the Kelly house. He told Aaron he was Mr. Kelly and he locked himself out. After we got him calmed down, I remembered his ability to draw pictures. He was able to draw a detailed picture of the man. We're getting it out to all the officers working on this case. He was released with the apologies of the Sheriff's Department. Jack just dropped me off at home for some clean clothes. Once I get a duffel bag packed, I'm going to be going back over to Donna Kelly's house."

"I don't like you staying there," Mark insisted. "It's too dangerous for you. You've been hurt once during this investigation. I don't want it to happen again."

She was glad she left out the part about the rock being thrown through the picture window. There was no need to give Mark anything more to worry about.

"If the response time when someone was trying to break in is any indication, I'm perfectly safe. How's Kitty holding up?"

"She's like me, a basket case. I'll let you talk to her. Just remember I love you and I want you to stay safe."

Mark's last comment took Rhonda by surprise. She knew her husband was completely faithful and concerned. Given the circumstances, someone could conclude what he said was a confession of guilt. As soon as the thought crossed her mind, Rhonda dismissed it. She knew Mark loved her and was genuinely worried about her.

Kitty came on the line and Rhonda listened as she voiced the same concerns as Mark had moments earlier.

"Hopefully, all of this will be over by the time Brad and Donna get back from their trip," Rhonda said, hoping her tone was reassuring. "We're following up on some solid leads. Something should break soon."

They talked all the while Rhonda packed her duffel. Within minutes of ending the conversation, Jack pulled into the driveway.

"I got the book you wanted. Don't know if it will be of much use to you. Bob Calloway at the funeral home said some people didn't take the time to sign it. I don't know why not. It would have certain been a diversion considering how long everyone had to wait to get through the line."

Rhonda could feel her hopes being dashed. What if the two young couples she wanted to investigate were some of the ones who didn't sign the book?

Once back at the Kelly house, they found Paul sitting at the kitchen table, surrounded by several books resembling journals he found in the floor safe.

"This guy had to be the world's greatest lover or a real bastard," Paul greeted them. "Unfortunately, he doesn't name names, he just gives them numbers. Of course, he describes everything from the weather to the location of where they had sex, to rating his lovers from one to ten."

Rhonda laughed at Paul's comment. It was true though; Karl was every man's perception of himself. The difference between Karl and Joe Blow off the street, was that Karl followed through on his fantasies.

When Paul asked about Aaron, she let Jack take over the narrative. The rumbling of her stomach reminded her it was after three and lunch had been forgotten.

Wandering over to the refrigerator, she took a ham sandwich out of the box sent to the house by the church after the luncheon. With any luck, it was still fresh enough to be eaten.

Once she was relaxed, Rhonda became aware of the ache in her head. With all the earlier excitement, the pain had been momentarily forgotten. In the hope of easing the pain, as soon as she finished her sandwich, we went into the living room to lie down on the couch. She'd hardly closed her eyes than she fell into a deep sleep.

~ * ~

"Have you received any more calls?" Jack asked Paul once Rhonda went into the living room to lie down.

"You know I did. They come on a regular basis, about ten to fifteen minutes apart."

Jack nodded. He was certain Paul understood the gravity of the situation, but at the same time, he doubted the young officer's judgement.

"You said Aaron drew a picture of the guy who asked him for help. I've heard he's quite the artist, but was it anything we can use in the investigation?"

Jack reached into his pocket and pulled out the copy of the picture Aaron drew. "See what you think."

He watched as Paul smoothed out the paper and stared at the drawing intently. "If I didn't know better, I'd say this was Reid Blake."

"Who's Reid Blake?"

"He's a guy who went to high school with me. Of course, I doubt it could be him."

Jack knew Paul wasn't a local kid, but for the life of him, he couldn't remember where Paul came from. "Where did you go to school?"

Paul named a small town just over the Illinois border.

"How well did you know Blake?"

Paul thought for a moment before answering. "About as well as I knew most of my classmates. He was a jock. I was a nerd. We didn't run in the same social circles, end of story."

Jack silently questioned Paul's statement about not being a jock. The man worked out regularly and had a muscular build.

"Do you remember anything else about him?"

"It seems to me his mother was divorced and his dad lives somewhere in another state. Of course, that wasn't anything new. Most of the rich kids in school were from broken families. You know how it goes, both parents try to buy the kid's love and mess up whatever values might have ever existed."

"Any idea where good old Reid might be now?"

Paul shook his head. "We had our tenth class reunion last summer and as I recall, he never responded. If I had the booklet from the reunion with me, I'd be able to give you the address they listed for him."

Since this was the first solid lead they'd had, Jack insisted Paul go over to his apartment and retrieve the book. If nothing else, it would give them a starting point for their investigation.

~ * ~

The house was strangely silent when Rhonda finally woke up. The events of the day had been draining to say the least, but she hadn't expected to sleep so long. She wondered where Paul was, since the constant drone of the television was non-existent.

Stretching, she got up from the couch and made her way to the kitchen. Once there, she saw Paul and Jack looking over some papers.

"What's up?" she asked, causing both of them to look

106

up at her.

"We've had our first lead," Jack said, handing her several sheets of paper that had been stapled together.

To her surprise, a graduation picture of a younger version of the man in Aaron's sketch looked back at her.

"How did you get this picture? Who is this guy? "

Her glance traveled over to the name, Reid Blake, listed beside the picture. Although there was an address listed for the man, there was no other information.

"I went to high school with him. I recognized him as soon as I saw Aaron's sketch. Luckily, the people who put together the class reunion had too much time on their hands. I was surprised to see our senior pictures beside each of our names in the booklet."

"Do you know if this is a current address?"

"While you were sleeping, I called one of the girls from the committee. She assured me that as of last summer it was a good address. In other words, the invitation to the reunion didn't come back as undeliverable. We've already turned the information over to the county as they have more resources than we do."

Rhonda felt cheated. She was glad she'd thought to bring her laptop from home. At least she could do a little digging on her own about this guy. Rather than begin to search the web, she absently picked up the funeral guest book that also sat on the table. She knew Jack thought she'd completely lost her mind in asking for it, but she was certain it had to contain some good information.

Even without her notes, she remembered the names of the people who stood in front of and behind the two couples she couldn't identify. Reading through the list of names she finally came across the first one she was looking for.

Beneath the names of Jim and Carolyn Meyer, were the two names she was hoping to find. The first, Karen and Michael Covington were written in the perfect script of a woman's delicate hand. The next names, Norman and Josie Ford, were far from neat and much harder to read. Unfortunately, neither couple listed an address in the space designated for it.

"Did you find what you were looking for?" Jack asked.

Rhonda finished writing down the names before looking up at her boss.

"Partially. There were four young couples who didn't seem to belong. I saw them come in, but they didn't stay together. These two went ahead of the others." She pointed at the names she'd found. "Hopefully, I can do enough research to find out their connection to the Reedman family."

"Speaking of connections," Paul began, "Has anyone found Susan Barclay yet?"

"There's been no word of her," Jack replied. "It's as though the ground opened and swallowed her whole. With what happened to Kitty, I can't say I blame her for disappearing."

Rhonda harbored a completely different concept of what happened to Susan. She hadn't liked the woman from the beginning and her disappearance made Rhonda distrust her more than ever. It was extremely interesting the last time Kitty heard from her friend was the morning after the murder. Since they left the police station, no one saw or heard anything from Susan. Kitty said Susan wanted to grieve in private and, therefore left her alone. To Rhonda that was a line of bull, especially since Susan hadn't attended either the visitation or the funeral.

"Well, I'll be damned."

Paul's exclamation jolted Rhonda back from her private mental ramblings.

"That conceited son of a bitch had the balls to sign his name to the guest register, along with his current address."

Rhonda took the book from Paul's hands and stared at the entry, Reid, and Anita Blake. The address listed a small town in Nebraska, with the same street name and number as in Paul's booklet from the class reunion.

"Well, that gives us more information to check out," Jack said. "I'll call it into the county right away."

Rhonda fumed. "I'm not ready to turn this over to the county so quickly. Let's do some of our own investigation on this first. It's as much our case as it is theirs. They wouldn't have half the information they do if it hadn't been for us."

"Don't you mean if it hadn't been for you?" Jack questioned.

"Okay, if it hadn't been for me. I was the one who called in the arson as well as the shots fired. I was also the one to suggest having Aaron see if he could draw a picture of the man who asked him for help. We aren't the idiots the county wants to make us out to be. I'm all for some of our own investigation on this one before we turn it over to them."

Jack gave her one of those looks that indicated he thought she was overstepping her boundaries but made no verbal comment.

"We were just thinking of ordering pizzas," Paul said, changing the subject. "Do you have any suggestions?"

Rhonda remembered the amount of food in the refrigerator left over from the funeral and brought over by the neighbors for the grieving family. "There's a ton of food in the refrigerator. I can't see letting it go to waste."

What she didn't say was how picky she'd become over her pizza. Maybe it was growing up most of her evening meals consisted of either pizza or burgers and fries from McDonalds.

Jack quickly excused himself, saying his wife was expecting him to take her out for fish. The mention of a good fish fry made Rhonda's mouth water. Until Jack made mention of it, she'd completely forgotten it was Friday, exactly one week since Karl Reedman's murder turned all their lives upside down.

Chapter Thirteen

"I think I've got something," Paul's voice came over the intercom.

Rhonda set aside the journal she'd been reading and hurried down to the lower level. The features of this house never ceased to amaze her. With the intercom system hooked up to each phone, family members could stay in touch with each other when necessary.

"I didn't mean to interrupt you," Paul said, when she stepped into the office.

"The only thing you interrupted was reading over and over again about all of Karl's sexual conquests."

Paul laughed at her description of the journals they'd taken turns reading over the last twenty-four hours.

"Just for shits and giggles, I went on Facebook and checked out the posts for Reid. Low and behold, if I didn't find chatter between him and two of the mystery people from the funeral registry."

Rhonda's heart raced. Her hunch paid off. Along with the three names she already knew, there were screen names with avatars rather than pictures. One was merely Reedman's Son and the second one listed herself as Sexy Diva.

The first post from the archives hit Rhonda like a punch in the gut.

I'm Karl Reedman's son and I know I must not be the only one. If that bastard got your mother pregnant, I want to know. Basically, I'm looking for the brothers and sisters I never knew.

From there the posts flew fast and furious. They covered everything from growing up as Karl Reedman's bastard kids to how unfair it was that the support ended once they became adults. From what she gathered, each of his kids had been supported until the age of eighteen, then given access to a trust fund for a college education. A mental calculation told her there would have been more than enough money for college, with the remainder coming to these kids at the age of twenty-five.

All the responders seemed to be well educated with high profile careers. Only Reedman's Son and Sexy Diva remained aloof without giving away too much information.

She followed the thread of the conversations from the stage where the players were getting acquainted, to the actual planning of the murder. Based on what she read, they all met in March to get to meet face to face but also to plan the dirty deed.

After reading about the plot, Rhonda concluded that Reedman's Son and Sexy Diva were the main instigators.

"I'd love to know who those two are," she said. "They seem to be the ones behind this whole thing."

"I've got the name of the hotel in Milwaukee where they met to plan the murder. The way this reads, they were all in attendance, except for Reedman's Son and Sexy Diva. It's one thing to use a screen name and an avatar on Facebook, but they'd have to use a real name to register at the hotel. Maybe Jack can work with the county to get us a subpoena for the hotel's registration records."

The thought of bringing the county in on what Rhonda now considered 'her' investigation galled her, but Paul had a good point. In order to get a subpoena, they would have to go through one of the county court judges and the sheriff's office would have more clout than Jack.

"I don't know what you think," Paul commented. "It looks to me as though they've set this up to look like one of those games on Facebook. In the last few posts, it says they're playing 'Killville'."

Rhonda took a closer look, then scrolled back down to the earlier posts. Before she'd been too interested in the content, she'd neglected to pay attention to the subject lines for many of the posts.

She scrolled back up to the more recent posts. The one that caught her eye came from Reid.

The deed is done. How good it was to hold that bastard's dick in my hands.

A post followed it almost immediately from Sexy Diva.

Don't forget he's not the only one standing in our way. There's the wife, the daughter, and the son.

The post continued giving the addresses for each of their homes.

"Whoever this woman is, she certainly knows a lot about the family," Rhonda said, stifling a yawn.

"Don't do that," Paul cautioned, yawning broadly. "Anyone would think we didn't get enough sleep last night. I do agree with you, though, this person does know a lot about the family. I'm not completely convinced Sexy Diva is a woman. It could be a disgruntled employee," Paul said, yawning again, reminding Rhonda how tired she also felt. "Besides, most of the information she gave is available on the Internet."

"Not the addresses," Rhonda argued.

"Why not? All it takes is a little digging on the right sites and magically, you can find almost anyone."

Rhonda wanted to ask Paul more questions, but her eyelids were so heavy she could no longer fight the urge to go to sleep.

~ * ~

Jack pushed the garage door opener in order to gain entrance to the Kelly house. From outside, he heard the drone of a lawnmower. *The sound of summer,* he thought as he shut out the noise by closing the overhead door. He'd just gotten a piece of information he knew Rhonda and Paul would be interested in hearing.

Stepping into the kitchen, he immediately sensed something was wrong. The sound of an alarm of some kind sounded, sending a sense of dread through his mind. Walking through the house, he found the kitchen as well as the living room deserted. The further he walked into the house, the more obnoxious the noise became. It took him a couple of moments to realize it came from the carbon monoxide detector. After he opened the kitchen window, he covered his mouth and nose with the handkerchief his wife insisted he carry, he made his way down to the lower lever where the office and fitness room were located.

He almost tripped over Rhonda's prone body when he entered the office and saw Paul slumped over the computer. Whatever set off the alarm, he was certain it had something to do with his two unconscious officers.

Making certain to keep his mouth and nose covered, he started opening windows on the lower lever as he had in the kitchen. Once he knew fresh air was coming into the house, he called dispatch to have an ambulance sent to the house immediately.

With the call completed, he dragged both Rhonda and Paul out the door onto the patio. As soon as she started breathing fresh air, Rhonda began to cough, but Paul remained unresponsive.

By the time the EMT's arrived, Rhonda was awake and alert but the same couldn't be said for Paul.

"What happened?" Rhonda questioned.

"The house is filled with carbon monoxide," Jack explained. "If I hadn't come when I did, I have no doubt the two of you would be dead. I've called for a Hazmat team to go through the house and try to figure out where it came from. For now, we're shutting down the surveillance. I refuse to put your lives in more danger over this."

Before Rhonda could protest, the EMT's finished checking out Paul and came over to take her vitals. Jack was grateful for the interruption, since it gave her a chance to digest what he said without flying off the handle at his suggestion.

Convinced his officers were in good hands, he went around to the front to the house to meet with the Hazmat team.

"Do you have any idea where the carbon monoxide came from?" he asked.

"When we arrived, we found a riding lawn mower running next to the intake valve for the air conditioner on the side of the house. That would be enough to get the carbon monoxide inside the house. Then it easily spread through the vents. Now that the house has been opened, the gas is dissipating."

Jack nodded. He recalled hearing the lawn mower, but never associated it with this house. In a neighborhood like this, it was entirely possible someone was mowing their lawn. Having received the all-clear to enter the house, he went in to check the answering machine. He listened to several taunting messages before he hit paydirt.

"Soon it will be nighty-night time. There's now three down and only one left to go."

The message was chilling to say the least.

Dread nibbled at the fringes of Jack's mind. With this latest information, he knew the next target would be Brad. He prayed that after the vandalism incident, the Denver Police Department was keeping a close watch not only on Brad's house but also his office. With only the law enforcement agencies involved in the investigation knowing about Karl Reedman's children being out of the country, it was possible these people could target Brad next.

~ * ~

The thought of going to the emergency room twice in one week irritated Rhonda no end. Of course, she understood the necessity, but it was still embarrassing. Before she was transported to the hospital, the EMT adjusted the oxygen mask covering her mouth and nose to give her the maximum of sweet clean air.

As the ambulance pulled away, she closed her eyes, but she didn't sleep. Her mind ran rampant with the information they'd gleaned over the past few hours. Even if Jack didn't allow her to return to the Kelly house, she had enough information stored in her mind to continue to investigate from home.

She made a mental note to make a list of the things she would need brought to her home. With luck, Jack would allow her to go in and retrieve them for herself. The last thing she needed was for her boss to be going through her clothes, including her undergarments. Just the thought of Jack touching her things made her skin crawl.

She'd just finished being checked out and dressing, when Jack entered her cubicle. "I've come to take you home," he said.

"Good, I'll be glad to get out of here. I heard someone say they admitted Paul. How bad is it?"

Jack's expression changed dramatically as he shook his head. "He's still unconscious. They've taken him up to ICU. For some reason the chemicals in the gas affected him more than they did you."

Rhonda tried to visualize the office where they'd been when they first started feeling sleepy. "Is it safe to go back into the house?"

"I talked to the Hazmat people, and they assured me the fresh air dissipated most of the gas. Why do you want to go back there?"

"For starters I need to get my stuff, but the main reason

is to get the notes Paul was making about what we found on the Internet. We got some great leads there that I can follow through on at home. I also want to check out the vents in the office. My memory is a little fuzzy at this point, but I think the air conditioning vent was positioned directly over the chair where Paul was sitting. If that's so, he would have breathed a more concentrated amount of it than me."

"It makes sense. I was afraid you would want to go back there and pick up where you left off."

"That's as dead a crime scene as the mansion. What are they saying about today's attack?"

"Just that one person is dead, and one is in ICU. They aren't releasing any names. At least it will keep our boy interested and around. What I was coming over to tell you this morning is that Reid Blake was registered at the Holiday Inn on the highway. He checked out yesterday morning, just before the incident with Aaron."

"Damn we missed him by a day. How long was he there?"

"The clerk said he and his wife checked in on Thursday of last week and she checked out Wednesday morning. That means she was here for the murder and the visitation. We've contacted the authorities in Nebraska, and they've issued a warrant for her arrest. Now all we need to do is find out who else is in on this."

"I need to do some more digging, but from what we've learned, there were six conspirators."

"Six? Where did you get that?"

"Before we got sick, Paul was looking into Reid's Facebook account. The posts made it look like they were playing a game called Killville, but the only players were one man, and one woman from each couple we identified from the visitation. The other two were someone identified as Reedman's Son and another known as Sexy Diva. It sounds like the last two were the ringleaders."

Jack gave her a bewildered look. "I've heard people talking about Facebook, but I don't have the slightest idea what it's all about."

If the situation hadn't been so dire, she would have laughed at Jack's ignorance of the Internet. "It's a networking tool. You set up a page and invite people to join you. After that you talk about anything and everything that's going on in your life."

"So, how do you plan a murder on a social network?"

"I need to do more research, but like I said before they started their own game called Killville. Between that and all the emails it came together quite easily."

Jack pulled into the garage and quickly hit the button to close the door before either of them got out of the car. Inside the house, everything was just as they had left it hours earlier, giving no sign of the drama leading up to the evacuation.

While Jack closed the open windows to keep out the predicted rain, Rhonda went from room to room collecting her belongings and putting them into her duffel before going down to the lower-level office. Once there, she seated herself at the desk. Looking up, she saw the air conditioning vent directly overhead.

"This was where Paul was sitting. Most of the time I was standing behind him so I could see what was on the computer screen."

She turned her attention to the desk, since the computer screen went black from non-use. Without disturbing any of the papers still on the desk, she picked up the legal pad Paul used to make his notes.

"I don't think there's anything else here I need," she finally declared. "I'm more than ready to go home and rest."

Jack looked relieved. "You're off the duty roster for the next week so that should give you plenty of recuperation time."

Rhonda tried to mask her enthusiasm. With the time off,

she'd be able to do some investigating on her own.

"Since that's the case, I think I'll go up to the lake and join Mark. It will be easier to relax away from all this madness."

Jack's smile said volumes as they went back up the stairs to go out to the garage.

Chapter Fourteen

Jack dropped Rhonda off at the house and told her he'd keep in touch through her cell phone.

She had no more than stepped into the living room when the phone began to ring.

"Oh, Jack, give me a break," she said aloud before answering. She didn't even check the caller ID.

The voice on the other end was chilling. *"Did you think you fooled us? Where do you have Donna stashed? We know she's not at the house."*

Rather than listening to more of what he had to say, she hung up. Using the house phone, she placed a call to Mark.

"I'm on my way up to the lake to be with you and Kitty," she announced as soon as Mark picked up the phone. "Don't try calling me on my cell. I'm not going to have it on. I'll see you in a couple of hours."

"What's going on, honey?"

"There's too much to go into at this point. I'll tell you everything when I get there. It will probably take me a little longer, especially if anyone is following me."

"Do you think you'll be followed?"

"I don't know, but I'm not taking any chances."

After hanging up on Mark, she called Jack. "I'm turning off my cell phone and leaving it at the house."

"Why?" Jack questioned.

"I was just contacted by one of the callers we have on tape. I'll give you the combination for the garage door and you can pick it up."

"That's not acceptable. Don't do anything until I get there. I'm sure you don't have the call recorded, but I don't want you pulling your vehicle out of the garage."

She took the time waiting for Jack to pack a bag and get ready to leave the house. She'd calculated how long it would take him and was surprised when he took much longer than she expected.

"What took you so long?" she asked as soon as he walked into the house.

"I stopped and picked up a cell phone we had at the office. It would work with your charger. I don't want you taking off without one. For all intents and purposes, I'm taking you into protective custody. At least that's what the report on the news will be. I've already contacted the sheriff's department. Once there, they will have a car you can take that won't be recognized. No one will know it's you driving away. I want you to keep in touch with us. If they've targeted you, they could do the same for Paul."

"Have you heard anything about him?"

She knew it was too soon to expect answers, but she couldn't help asking.

"I checked with the hospital. They told me there's been no change in his condition. I contacted his parents and they're on their way. What I don't understand is why the people behind this called you and how they got your cell phone number?"

"I don't either, but they do know Donna and Sean weren't in that house. The guy who called told me he knew we had Donna stashed somewhere and wanted to know where. I hung up without answering his questions. If these people are true to form, they'll keep up the calls constantly."

"I totally agree with you. Are you ready to go?"

Rhonda nodded and picked up her suitcase. She didn't need much, since she knew her, mother-in-law kept a complete wardrobe at the lake house. She was glad she'd put her laptop in the suitcase, since there would be no need for her to take it with her to the jail when they took her into protective custody.

Sheriff Cantwell met them as soon as they arrived at the jail. "I hope this plan of yours works, Franks."

"So, do I. I have Rhonda's cell phone turned off so we can get all the messages. From what she told me they know Donna is out of town. We need to get Rhonda to a safe place as soon as possible. I've given her a different cell phone to use and by taking a car from here, we hope she won't be followed."

"Maybe putting her in protective custody isn't such a bad idea," Sheriff Cantwell suggested.

"It most certainly is a bad idea," Rhonda protested. "I have a place to go and people are expecting me. Besides, if I'm in jail, I can't do the research I need to do on this case."

"What research?" Sheriff Cantwell questioned.

"Just something Paul and I stumbled on while we were at Donna and Sean's place. I don't want to say much about it at this point, since it could turn out to be a bad lead. If it turns out to be productive, I'll let you know."

The sheriff seemed to take her explanation at face value, but she knew Jack didn't believe a word she'd said. While the sheriff went to get the keys to a car she could use, Jack turned to her.

"You're really onto something here. I trust you to follow through with it. You know, I have enough trouble with my email to say nothing about trying to do any digging on the Internet."

Before she could reply, the sheriff returned with the keys to an Escalade confiscated in a drug raid. Just in case anyone is watching, we have a wig and a dress for you to wear. I don't put anything past these people. They seem to be intent on getting you out of the way."

Rhonda agreed and went into the bathroom to change her appearance drastically. The wig was a short gray style, and the dress made her look more like a matronly woman than an experienced officer, especially with the padding she wore under it. That along with the cane the sheriff gave her, made the disguise complete.

"I doubt my husband would recognize me dressed like this," she said when she finally emerged from the bathroom.

Within half an hour, Rhonda was on the Interstate heading north. Stopping at the first rest stop she came to; she breathed a sigh of relief to know no one followed her at the exit. Once inside the restroom, she changed her clothes and took off the padding that was far too hot to wear any longer. After getting back into the car, she called Mark to tell him about what she would be driving so he could keep an eye out for her. She also gave him the new cell phone number where she could be reached. With the call completed, she pulled back onto the highway and readied herself for the remainder of the trip.

~ * ~

Mark and Kitty were on the porch waiting for Rhonda when she finally pulled into the driveway. She was glad she could finally turn off the ignition of the parked car. Her head ached, not only from the place where the rock hit, but also from the effects of the carbon monoxide she'd inhaled at the Kelly house.

"Thank God you're here where I can keep an eye on you," Mark said, rushing over to the car and lifting her high in the air. "Are you sure you weren't followed."

"Positive. They made a news release saying I'd been taken into protective custody. Once I got to the jail, I dressed up like an old woman and drove away in this vehicle. While I was changing, they put my suitcase in the car before they pulled it out of the police garage. It was all very James Bondish. I felt like I was in a cloak-and-dagger movie rather than real life."

"This isn't as innocent as you want us to believe. I've

been worried about your safety ever since they firebombed the mansion," Kitty said, coming off the porch to embrace Rhonda. "At least you're here and we know you're safe."

Rhonda sobered. "I wish I could say the same for Paul."

"What about Paul?" Mark asked.

"He was at the Kelly house with me when somehow carbon monoxide got into the ventilation system. He's in intensive care. I came out of the stupor it put me in right away, but the last I heard, he was still unconscious. It doesn't sound good. He must have gotten more of it in his lungs than I did, since he was sitting right under the vent."

Kitty began to cry. Rhonda knew it was hard for her to understand not only what had brought about her husband's murder, but also the attempt on her life as well as the one on Donna and Sean's lives. Now another life was threatened.

~ * ~

Rhonda didn't know how much the events of the day exhausted her until she stretched out on the couch in the living room of the lake house. Dreamless sleep came immediately and was only interrupted by the ringing of the cell phone in her pocket. After the incident this morning, she automatically checked the caller ID. Relieved to see Jack's name and number displayed, she answered.

"I wanted to make certain you made it there safely," he greeted her.

From the tone of his voice, she knew there was something he wasn't telling her. "What's wrong?" she inquired.

After a moment of silence, Jack cleared his throat. "Paul passed away about half an hour ago. He never regained consciousness. Since our killers know Donna wasn't at the house, we're releasing the details of Paul's death along with the information of you being taken into protective custody."

Tears rolled down Rhonda's cheeks at the news about Paul. It certainly didn't embarrass her, as Jack was crying as well. This escalated from a horrific murder to terrifying threats, to killing one of the police department's own.

"I'll keep you posted," Jack promised, when he realized Rhonda was too choked up to reply. "If there's somewhere you can stash that Escalade, I'd do so. There's no use in advertising there's a strange car at you in-law's place."

"It's already done," she managed to choke out.

With the phone call ended, she went into the kitchen to find Mark and Kitty.

"We thought you'd sleep longer, honey," Mark said before he turned to take her in his arms. "What's wrong? You're crying."

"Paul died without regaining consciousness. It should have been me. I'm the one who was investigating this crime. He was just along for the ride. We should have gotten out of that house after all the stuff that happened yesterday."

"You couldn't have known," Kitty assured her. "None of this makes any sense whatsoever."

Mark guided Rhonda to one of the chairs at the kitchen table, then poured her a glass of lemonade. Only when she was seated did she realize the table was set for supper.

"Mark is fixing fish on the grill and I'm in charge of the frozen French fries along with my kick ass coleslaw," Kitty said.

Rhonda took a long sip of her lemonade, realizing Mark had added some vodka to it. *How like him to know I needed something stiffer than straight lemonade.* The cool vodka laced lemonade reminded Rhonda just how hungry she'd become.

"Are there any leads?" Mark asked after they finished eating.

"Just something I want to check out further. It seems that Aaron was able to do a sketch of the man who asked him for help."

Mark laughed. "I have no doubts about that. The kid is quite an artist. Remember the picture he drew of us at the neighborhood picnic last year?"

"That's why I suggested he draw the picture for the deputies. It turned out Paul recognized the guy in the picture as a classmate of his from high school. After checking the guest book from the visitation and the funeral, we found he signed the book using his full name and address. This guy's name is Reid Blake."

Rhonda watched Kitty's reaction to the name. "That's a name I'm not likely to forget. He came to the house about six months ago asking for a job. Karl asked for a resume, but he told him at the time he didn't have any openings. The meeting ended with the man calling Karl a bastard. Do you think that's why Karl was murdered?"

"I doubt it," Rhonda replied. "I think the motive goes deeper than that. We've found out Reid Blake was one of Karl's out-of-wedlock kids. So far, we've identified two others, but there is still one we can't find. There are also two others we can't put names to. They met each other on Facebook. That's what we were researching when we were overcome with the carbon monoxide."

Tears filled Kitty's eyes. "I knew there was something bothering Karl. He said some of the kids he'd fathered tried to contact him, but it wasn't anything I should worry about."

"I think he was more worried than you thought. He mentioned it in his journal. I had Jack bring over the safe to the house and Paul was able to get it open. Once he did, we found the current journal along with several other papers. We found the backdated journals in the safe at his office, but he didn't kiss and tell. He gave the women he slept with numbers and rated them from one to ten."

Kitty nodded. "I knew he did. My number was fifty-two-forty-two, and my rating was ten plus. He just picked the numbers arbitrarily but not the ratings. The numbers didn't mean anything. I think he kept a master list on his computer. Of course, it was in the library and probably destroyed in the fire."

Rhonda knew it was a long shot, but she planned to have Jack go out to the mansion and see if he could find the CPU and get anything off the hard drive.

"Let's see what they have to say on the evening news," Mark suggested, changing the subject.

Rhonda and Kitty got up from the table and followed Mark into the living room. After Mark turned on the TV, he chose a Madison station with local news.

"On the local front, the Reedman murders are again in the headlines. As we reported yesterday, several attacks have taken place at the home of Sean and Donna Kelly. Donna Kelly is the daughter of the late Karl Reedman, the murdered millionaire. Fortunately, the Kelley's are vacationing out of the country and two city officers, Rhonda Pohs and Paul Roberts, were occupying the house.

"We've received word that this morning, there was a chemical attack on the house and its occupants. Officer Pohs was treated and released and is now in protective custody, Unfortunately, Officer Roberts died of Carbon Monoxide poisoning, late this afternoon. At this hour, the manhunt continues. Anyone with information regarding this case is asked to call Crime Stoppers at 608 555-STOP. That's 608 555-7867."

"Well, that certainly tips our hand, doesn't it?" Ronda commented. "Of course, someone already knows I'm involved. The call I received on my cell today confirms that, They know who I am, but they certainly don't think I know their identity. We tracked Blake to the Holiday Inn on the highway, but he checked out last night. Jack is checking the other hotels in the area."

"That makes sense," Mark commented. "Something

tells me this guy isn't sleeping in his car. Since he's from out of state, I'm willing to bet he's using a rental. Why don't you check out the rental companies? Maybe you can find out what he's driving."

Mark's suggestion had merit. While Kitty cleared the table, Rhonda began calling various car rental companies. She finally got a positive response. According to the company located at the Madison airport, Reid Blake rented a red Chrysler convertible. She even obtained the license plate number so Jack could put an APB.

~ * ~

Although Jack hoped Rhonda would take some time to rest, he knew she couldn't let go of this case. Her getting the description of the car Blake rented, along with the license plate number, tightened the noose on their prime suspect.

Even though it was late, Jack remained at the office. With Rhonda in hiding and the loss of Paul Roberts, he was running short-handed.

Was it just a week ago when this was a quiet office? he wondered. *I'm beginning to think I'm too old for police work.*

The thought no more than crossed his mind when the phone on his desk began to ring. "Franks here," he answered.

"Jack, this is Cantwell. We have Blake in custody."

Jack's heart beat faster as adrenaline pumped through his system. "How did you catch him?"

"Much as I hate to admit it, that information Officer Pohs provided us helped. One of my deputies recognized the license plate number when he arrested him on the highway. He told Blake the reason he stopped him was for passing in a no-passing zone. As soon as my deputy read the name on the license, he arrested the suspect on three counts of murder. He's bringing him in right now. I thought you'd want to be in on the questioning."

Jack wished Rhonda was in town and could be there as well. He didn't like it, but knew he needed to go to the jail alone.

After calling his wife to tell her not to expect him home until much later, he grabbed his hat and prepared to leave the office. As much as he wanted a cigarette, he refrained from lighting up. He made it a practice not to smoke in his squad car, so having a cigarette while driving was out of the question. As much as he wanted one, he knew he needed to drive the eight miles to the jail as quickly as possible without breaking the speed limit. True he could go there with lights and sirens, but there was no point in drawing that much attention to himself.

"Blake asked for a lawyer as soon as we got him in the interrogation room," Cantwell said when Jack entered his office. "Considering he has an out-of-state license, it surprised me when he asked for someone from Madison."

"Who did he ask for?" Jack inquired.

"Some guy named Michael Covington. The name didn't mean anything to me, but we called the number for his office and were directed to his cell phone since it was the weekend. Mr. Covington assured us he'd be here within the hour."

The name Cantwell mentioned immediately set off warning bells in Jack's head. It matched one of the names from the visitation guest book Rhonda had been looking at. Since they hadn't made the information common knowledge, Jack decided not to say anything about it until he could talk to Rhonda. If this all played out the way he hoped, they would know where to find Mr. Covington.

Wanting a good look at the monster behind the mayhem of the past week, Jack walked to the one-way window looking into the interrogation room.

The man sitting at the table was a dead ringer for the picture Aaron drew. As much as Jack wanted to go in and wring the son of a bitch's neck, he refrained.

"Looks like the picture the kid drew, doesn't he?" Cantwell asked when he joined Jack.

"Sure does. It goes to show you Aaron is an excellent artist. He might have a good career in police work."

Cantwell looked at Jack skeptically.

"What I mean is he'd make a good sketch artist."

"I suppose, but I can't see the department ever hiring anyone with a mental handicap."

Jack's blood boiled. "Aaron's not as handicapped as you think. He has Down's Syndrome. There's a big difference."

"Just where are you holding my client?" a well-dressed man demanded as he crossed the room to where Jack and Cantwell were standing.

"If you're referring to Reid Blake, he's in this interrogation room."

Cantwell motioned toward the one-way window so the man could get a good look at Blake.

"You local yokels do know enough not to listen to my conversation with my client, don't you?"

"We may be local, but we do know the law," Jack spat. "Your conversation with Mr. Blake will be strictly confidential. Just be aware, he's charged with three counts of murder in the first degree."

Covington glared at Jack before entering the interrogation room.

"Weren't you a little hard on him, Jack? He is an officer of the court, you know."

"I need to talk to Rhonda on this, but I think Covington's in this up to his eyebrows. If I'm not mistaken, his name is the same as one of the people she's been investigating."

He went on to explain about the Facebook connection with Blake and the other co-conspirators.

"If that's so, we should arrest him."

129

"Not so fast. If he's a lawyer, he's not going anywhere. Until we tie together all the information, we shouldn't tip our hand. Let's give them enough rope to hang themselves. It's wise not to divulge too much information until we know more about the rest of the conspirators."

Cantwell looked at him with surprise at this new insight. Hell, he couldn't take any credit for his information. That belonged to Rhonda. As he thought about her, Jack knew he had to give her the information on this latest development in this case.

~ * ~

Rhonda was just getting ready for bed when her cell phone rang. Since Jack and Mark were the only ones to know the number, she didn't hesitate in answering.

"Great news," Jack announced without even saying hello. "We've arrested Blake and you'll never guess who his lawyer is."

Rhonda smiled. With the research she'd been doing all evening she had a pretty good idea. "Let's see, it wouldn't be Michael Covington, would it?"

"That's right, how did you know?"

"Mark and I have been very busy on the computer. I've been going through the Facebook accounts and Mark has been searching for names. He just found out that Covington is a practicing lawyer in Madison. Of course, Blake won't be able to rely too heavily on him, since his specialty is real estate law. You aren't planning to arrest him, are you?"

Jack chuckled. "Cantwell wanted to, but I told him what you said. Guess he agreed with you, since he dropped the objections when I mentioned your name."

"Are you going to be in on the questioning?"

"I doubt it. Something tells me Covington will advise him to keep his mouth shut. He's been Mirandized and will probably be arraigned first thing Monday morning. I thought you might want to be in court. I know it's a long drive, but Mark could come with you."

Chapter Fifteen

For most of Sunday, Rhonda and Mark spent their time on the computer, trying to glean as much information as possible. Even though they hadn't been able to identify either Sexy Diva or Reedman's Son, they compiled enough information on the co-conspirators to put them away for the rest of their lives.

On the drive back to town, Rhonda felt apprehensive. What if someone figured out Kitty wasn't dead? If they did, would they think to look for her at the lake house? She prayed not.

"Are you sure Kitty will be alright?" she asked for the umpteenth time since leaving the lake.

"I'm positive. She's been alone at the house while I've been out on the lake. The arraignment won't take very long then we can head back. On the way to the courthouse, we'll stop off at the house and pick up the SUV. I get a little nervous about driving a vehicle that isn't ours."

Rhonda agreed. The Escalade has been fun to drive, but she would certainly feel more comfortable in their own vehicle.

At the courthouse, they found the prosecutor waiting for them. "Jack said you might show up for this, Rhonda."

She smiled as she recognized George Mathews. He'd grown up down the street from Rhonda's house and teased her unmercifully when they were kids. She knew he'd become a lawyer but hadn't realized he'd joined the prosecutor's office.

"Try keeping me away. This bastard killed not only Mr. and Mrs. Reedman, but also my partner. Of course, I don't think he acted alone. I have information linking several other people that I'll happily turn over to your office. I can identify the names of two couples but the other two are using screen names only. I need to try to figure out who they are."

"Do you have the information with you?"

Rhonda reached into her oversized purse and produced the printed sheets from the Facebook accounts for all the people involved.

"The ones I can't identify are Reedman's Son and Sexy Diva. They could be anyone, considering the number of affairs Karl Reedman had over the years. It's funny that after the murder, there were no more postings from Reedman's Son. The latest ones are from Sexy Diva. I have a feeling the two of them are the ring leaders."

"This could prove to be very interesting. Thanks Rhonda. I'm sure this is something I can use. Maybe it's enough to make Mr. Blake's attorney take a plea."

Rhonda saw two well-dressed men enter the courtroom. The first one she recognized from the funeral home, but the other was a stranger.

As the proceedings got underway, Blake's attorneys predictably pleaded their client not guilty.

When it was time for George to speak, he asked that Blake be held without bail, since being from out of state he should be considered a flight risk.

Rhonda was relieved when the judge agreed with George and refused to grant bail. Considering the charges lodged against Blake, it only made sense. Of course, there were only two murders, but neither Jack nor Rhonda was ready to tell the world Kitty was still alive, considering there were still at least three conspirators unaccounted for.

The two attorneys representing Blake left the courtroom to talk to George.

"You know this is a bunch of bull," Covington said as soon as he stood in front of George. "Our client is only here on vacation. Why are you harassing him?"

"Because we have evidence that he tried to break into the Kelly home, he's implicated in the murders of Karl as well as Kitty Reedman. It's entirely possible he's involved in the murder of Officer Paul Roberts."

"My client doesn't even know these people. I don't know why you think he's guilty."

"We have proof from his Facebook account showing he was involved in a game called Killville with a player by the name of Reedman's Son."

"That's only a game," Covington argued. "People play those games on Facebook all the time. I know my wife and I enjoy them."

"So, we've noticed. We see you're one of the registered players and you went to the visitation for Karl Reedman. Is there anything you want to tell us that could shed some light on this case?"

"Of course not. We were only playing a game. We went on that visitation because my wife went to school in this town. She knew Brad Reedman. She wanted to come to pay her respects to her high school friend."

"We think there's more to it than that. Would you and your wife be willing to give us a DNA sample?"

"I'll willingly give you a sample, but my wife is out of town on vacation with her sister. I'm sure you can understand she's not available."

Rhonda wanted to scream. She didn't believe a word of what this bastard was telling George, but she held herself in check.

"Thank goodness you were able to control your instincts. I was sure you were going to explode," George said, once the two of them were alone.

"It was hard not to say something. Do you think his wife is out of town?"

"Not for a minute. There are some things I need to tell you. For starters, we've arrested Blake's wife in Nebraska.

She'll be extradited to Wisconsin either Tuesday or Wednesday of this week. From what I've heard, she's naming names and giving the details of how the murder went down. That's the good part.

"The bad is that we've heard from the authorities in Aruba. Donna and her husband are missing. Brad reported them missing last night. They are looking into it. After that high school student went missing down there, they're giving this the VIP treatment."

"That's not all," Jack said as he joined them. "We've found Susan Barclay. She's out in Denver. The way you and Mark can work on the computer, is it possible you can find out anything more about her?"

"How did you find out she was in Denver?"

"We went back and talked to her secretary. The woman isn't a happy camper since she just got fired. Susan said it was too dangerous for her to stay in Wisconsin, so she relocated her practice to Colorado. It seems strange she would move to the same city as where Brad Reedman lives."

Rhonda recalled the vandalism to Brad's house the day after the funeral. It was entirely possible Susan Barclay and Sexy Diva were one in the same. If that was the case, she would be the one trying to get Brad out of the way for the rest of the Reedman bastards.

"Oh, my god," Rhonda gasped. "I was wrong. It doesn't matter who Reedman's Son is. Susan is behind all of this. She's Sexy Diva. I'm willing to bet money if you investigate Susan's background, or even check her DNA, we'll find she's one of Karl's bastards. It's possible she thought getting close to him would get her part of his money when he died. Unfortunately, she found out everything was being left to his legitimate kids. She might even have thought Kitty would be getting more than the trust fund he set up for her, since she was his current wife. It only makes sense. With Kitty dead, she must have thought the next one to die had to be Donna and now she's missing. I don't know how she pulled it off, but I'm concerned for Brad's safety."

"We are too," Jack said "So are the authorities in Aruba. They're keeping a close watch on him. It's more than a coincidence, since the Kelly's were lost at sea in a tragic boating accident. Brad told the police down there; Donna and Sean were using a boat that was at the condo where they were staying. When they didn't come back, he contacted the proper people. The only thing they were able to find was the overturned boat. There was no sign of Donna or Sean. I doubt they will ever find the bodies. Those waters are shark infested."

Rhonda's heart sank. Donna had such great plans for her life and now it was cut short. It made all the things that happened this past week pale in comparison. The only thing worse than her death was that of a fine young officer like Paul.

Chapter Sixteen

Rather than return to the lake, Rhonda insisted on staying at the house so she could be in on the questioning of Blake. Even though Mark wanted to stay with her, she insisted he go back to be with Kitty.

After spending two nights at home alone, she was, at last, at the jail for the interrogation.

"I must insist you not say anything, Mrs. Blake," said the attorney who represented Reid at the arraignment on Monday morning.

"Look, Mr. Jackson, I'm not happy about being here, but I refuse to remain silent any longer. I'm as much to blame as anyone else. I took part in the murder of Karl Reedman. If he had acknowledged his kids, things might have been different, but he didn't. Not only is Reid his son, so is Michael Covington. They were the ones who planned this with Reedman's Son and Sexy Diva. I didn't want to come along, but Reid insisted. After they cut off Karl's penis, they told all the women to pee on it.

"Everyone was there except for Reedman's Son. There was a woman there that we didn't know. She said she only wanted to be known as Sexy Diva. After it was done, we all stayed in town to go on the visitation, then I flew home. I was so appalled by what we'd done, I started divorce proceedings. I didn't want any of the blood money Reid stood to inherit."

"There was another couple there, did you know them?"

Anita shook her head no. "Reid called them Norman and Josie Ford, but I never knew what their connection could be."

Rhonda could feel her heart sink to the pit of her

stomach. Everything Anita was saying corresponded exactly with the way Rhonda imagined the murder taking place. The only missing pieces were the identities of Reedman's Son and Sexy Diva.

After leaving the county Jail, Rhonda went to talk to Jack and meet with Brad. Earlier, she'd received a call from Jack informing her Brad had returned to the states and was scheduled to arrive at the office in about fifteen minutes.

"I can't believe this could happen to my sister," she heard Brad say as she stood outside of Jack's office.

She knocked on the door and waited until Jack recognized her, so she could interrupt his conversation with Brad. "Rhonda, come on in," he called.

When she entered the room, she saw Bard face to face for the first time since the funeral. He looked tanned from his time spent in Aruba, but his eyes showed his lack of sleep. Instinctively, she extended her hand to him.

"I'm so sorry, Brad. This must be a terrible blow to your family. At least we have two of the men and two of the women involved in your father's murder in jail. What happened with Donna?"

"I was just telling Jack that she and Sean wanted to go sailing. When they didn't return, I contacted the authorities. Two hours later, their boat was found capsized about a mile out. They told me they doubted anyone would ever find their bodies."

"Will you be returning to Denver?"

"I don't think so, at least not for a while. From what Jack tells me there were several conspirators. Your having only caught a few of them doesn't make me feel comfortable. I don't think it would be safe for us to return home considering the vandalism to the house the day after the funeral."

Rhonda nodded in agreement. It would be foolish for Brad and his wife to put themselves in danger. Donna's tormentors were Reid Blake, Michael Covington, and Norman

Ford. With two of them in custody, it wouldn't be long before they found the third man. All that stood in the way of Brad trying to piece his life back together would be Sexy Diva and Reedman's son. Considering they had a good idea about the identity of Sexy Diva, it wouldn't be long before she was in custody as well.

"Besides," Brad continued, "I'm going to have to relocate here to keep Dad's business running. Jack was just telling me about the damage to Donna's place. It doesn't sound like it would take too much to make it livable, at least until I can get a contractor hired to restore the mansion."

Something about Brad's attitude didn't sit well with Rhonda. Maybe it was the fact she'd stayed in that house and everything about it screamed Donna and Sean. Maybe it was to admit that missing at sea equaled dead. Whatever it was, the thought of Brad and Loretta living in Donna's house didn't seem right. If it were her, she wouldn't want to stay in a dead woman's house and use her things.

"Will there be a funeral?" Rhonda asked.

"I'm planning a memorial service," Brad replied. "It will be not only for Donna and Sean but also for Kitty. With her burned in the fire, it's the same as Donna and Sean, there's nothing to bury, but she should be remembered. I do know my father loved her. I'm sorry, I must get back to Loretta. This has taken a terrible toll on her."

"Well," Jack said, "you know you have our sympathies. If there's anything we can do to help you, please don't hesitate to get in touch with us."

Brad showed a weak smile as he shook hands with both Jack and Rhonda before leaving.

"Something about this doesn't make sense to me. Would you be so quick to move into your dead sister's house?" Rhonda asked.

"That's funny, I was thinking the same thing. At the same time, he has to have somewhere to live, and I suppose he would be comfortable there. Since he's been working in the Denver office of his dad's business, it's only natural for him to come back here and take over. It's going to be a while before the mansion is livable. I guess staying at the Kelly house is better than having to rent a place. With Donna dead, he owns everything."

"Everything?"

"We've been doing some investigation, of our own, into Karl's holdings. It seems he owned not only the mansion but also the houses where Donna and Brad were living. I checked with the tax offices both here and in Denver. They confirmed Karl Reedman owned the houses and he was the one who paid the taxes. According to the will, everything would be split between Brad and Donna. With Donna dead, he gets both places free and clear. It would have been different if Donna and Brad had kids, but they didn't, so there is no one to contest Brad getting everything."

"Isn't that convenient? Of course, inheriting everything doesn't make him guilty of anything, but it gives him a good motive."

"You don't think Brad had anything to do with this, do you?"

"I don't know. He's a convenient victim, but somehow, I can't believe he's a co-conspirator. How are we coming on finding Norm and Josie Ford?"

Jack scratched his head. "We've hit a dead end. It's as though the two of them don't exist. As for Covington and Blake, they only know what they've read on Facebook about them. They all met in Milwaukee to plan the murder, but the Fords weren't very talkative about who they were or where they lived."

"What about Reedman's Son and Sexy Diva?"

"They're sticking to the story that although Sexy Diva was there, Reedman's Son wasn't. He did everything by phone, and they made it clear they all wanted Karl dead, along with his wife and both of his ligament kids. Until we find the other conspirators, we'll have to keep a close watch on Brad. It's no secret his life is in danger."

"I certainly wish I could get a DNA sample from Susan."

The look on Jack's face was one of complete defeat. "We've searched her office as well as her apartment. Both are as clean as a whistle. There wasn't even a tissue left in the waste basket."

Rhonda thought for a moment. "It's a good thing you have me on leave for the rest of the week. I'm going up to the lake to talk to Kitty. She might be able to tell me something I need to know, like if there is anything at the mansion we can use."

"The mansion? You can't get in there. Technically, it belongs to Brad."

Rhonda smiled broadly. "Technically, it's still a crime scene. He can't do anything until it's released. Make sure Sheriff Cantwell doesn't release anything until I get back. In the meantime, have you gotten the CPU?"

Jack looked at her sheepishly. She knew her request for the CPU was like the one for the safe. He'd agreed to do it, but other aspects of the case got in the way, and he'd forgotten.

"Never mind," she said, trying not to sound exasperated. "I'll stop out there on the way up to the lake. You're welcome to meet me there to bring it back to the county lab. Hopefully, they can find something on the hard drive we can use."

~ * ~

Rhonda stopped at the house to change into her old jeans and a pair of rain boots. With the mess at the mansion, she didn't want to ruin anything else she might wear.

She was pleased to see Jack's cruiser at the mansion

when she pulled into the driveway. She hadn't been here since the day of the firebombing and the devastation hit her hard.

"I can't believe I got here before you did," Jack greeted her.

"I went by the house to change my clothes. I never thought to get a pair of coveralls at the office."

She nodded the pair of coveralls Jack put on over his uniform.

"I don't like wearing these things, but I remembered how dirty it is in that rubble. If you're ready, let's go down to the lower level."

Rhonda followed Jack down the steep embankment of the hill the mansion had been built into. She was pleased there hadn't been any rain in the past week. At least the damage from the water used to fight the fire hadn't been compounded by a storm.

"It looks like everything from the library ended up in the swimming pool," Rhonda observed.

"I don't think we're going to find anything we can use. It's filled with water. Hopefully the CPU will not have sustained much damage."

Rhonda wasn't holding out much hope but headed toward the mess of debris that had once been the elegant library where she and Kitty shared iced tea and conversation just a little over a week ago.

"I don't believe it," Jack declared, causing Rhonda to look in his direction. "The CPU is over here. It didn't land in the pool at all."

Rhonda felt like a kid on Christmas morning. It was a miracle the CPU hadn't landed in the water of the swimming pool. She picked up a couple of other things, including a strong box resting on the side of the pool. This would give them something to investigate. The last thing she found was a silver frame with a picture of Kitty and Karl in it. Considering the background looked like one of the wedding chapels in Las

Vegas, she knew it had to be their wedding picture. This was something Kitty would want.

"Did you find anything else?" Jack inquired.

"Just this," she said handing him the strong box. "I also found a picture of Kitty and Karl in happier times. I'm going to take it to her. It has nothing to do with the crime scene. There isn't any reason I can't take it to her, is there?"

"None that I can see," Jack replied. "Let's get these things back up to the car. With luck, you can get up to the lake in time for dinner."

~ * ~

"I can't believe you found this strong box and picture. I was afraid the picture was lost forever. As for the strong box, it was where we kept our marriage license as well as some papers that were important to me."

"I'm glad I was able to bring it to you. What I need to know is if there is anything that might contain Susan's DNA at the mansion."

"Why are you looking for Susan's DNA?" Kitty asked, leaning back in the patio chair.

The last rays of the afternoon sun bathed the entire area in a bright light.

"She's disappeared completely. If you remember, one of the conspirators identified herself as Sexy Diva. That certainly describes Susan, don't you think?"

"It does, but where would she be?"

"That's what we don't know. Her office told us she was closing everything up and moving to Denver. The problem is even though she maintained a rented office and apartment in Denver everything has been completely cleaned out."

"I knew about the office in Denver," Kitty admitted. "It was her primary location, but she was in the process of completely relocating here. We talked about what a coincidence it was that she had an office in Denver and that was where Brad lived. Of course, it's a big city, not like here. I told her she was foolish to relocate completely, since she could make so much more money in Colorado than she did in Wisconsin. She said she loved both Karl and me. She couldn't stand being so far away from us."

"I understand, but we need to exonerate her in this case. Can you think of anything she might have left behind at the mansion?"

Kitty took a minute to obviously concentrate on the place that must have brought her so much happiness as well as sorrow.

"When she stayed over, Susan had the bedroom next to ours. You might find something there, but I doubt it. It's the one that's painted blue. I hope it helps to clear her name. She's one of the few female lovers I've had who could completely satisfy me."

The thought of two women making love turned Rhonda's stomach, but who was she to judge what others did behind closed doors? Kitty was very open about her sexual preferences. If it didn't bother Karl, it shouldn't have concerned her.

Chapter Seventeen

The next morning, Rhonda drove back to town and stopped at the police station before going back to her place.

"Are you up to another trip out to the mansion?" she asked once she entered Jack's office.

"Did you get some information we can use?"

"I most certainly did. I wanted to check things out before I get ready to go to Paul's funeral. Are you going?"

"I can't. We're running short handed here and I can't take the time off. I did go down for the visitation last night. It was emotional. I think every officer who wasn't on duty was there. His parents are devastated."

"I don't blame them."

Rhonda drove out to the mansion, followed by Jack in the squad car. It wasn't hard to find the bedroom Susan used when she spent nights with Karl and Kitty. In the adjoining bathroom, they found a lipstick, deodorant, a toothbrush, and a hair brush. In her hurry to clean everything out of her apartments and offices she forgot the things she left behind at the mansion.

"I'll get these to the lab, but you'd better be on your way. It's almost ten and the funeral is set for one this afternoon."

Rhonda agreed. After waiting for Jack to leave the mansion, she headed for home to change her clothes before going to the funeral.

~ * ~

As Jack predicted, the sanctuary was already filled,

leaving her no place to sit but in the back of the church on a folding chair. Speaker after speaker told of various aspects of Paul's life. When they asked if anyone else had anything to say, Rhonda found herself on her feet.

She waited until one of the ushers handed her a microphone before she began to speak. "Paul and I were partners on a murder case when he died. The people responsible for the previous murders thought we were someone else and they wanted them out of the way. Paul just found something we hoped would break the case wide open, when we were both overcome by carbon monoxide coming through the air conditioning system. He died a hero, serving in the line of duty. He will be missed by everyone on the force who ever worked with him."

Tears flowed down her cheeks and she began to shake. The man sitting next to her got to his feet and put his arm around her shoulders, before helping her to seat herself again.

"That was a moving tribute," he whispered, as others got up to speak.

"It was the truth. I thought people should know how he died. I was lucky. I didn't get the same amount of the gas he did by sitting closer to the vent. It should have been me, not him that died."

"Don't ever say that. It was Paul's' time. I've known since he was a kid; he wouldn't live a long life."

"You've known him that long?"

The man smiled and nodded. "I'm Anson Wallace. Paul was my nephew. He had cancer as a kid and beat it, only to get asthma when he was in his teens. I think it was under control, but it could account for the way the carbon monoxide affected him and not you. I'd like you to meet the rest of the family. You don't have to get right back, do you?"

Rhonda assured him, her time was her own and she'd be able to stay for the luncheon, since she was on medical leave.

"I'd be honored to meet Paul's family. He was a very special officer and his future with the department was bright."

Since Paul was going to be cremated once the coffin was closed, it was rolled away without the mandatory trip to the cemetery.

"Rhonda, these folks are Paul's parents," Anson said, making the necessary introductions.

"It's such a pleasure to meet you," Paul's mother said. "Paul spoke highly of you."

"He most certainly did," Paul's father agreed. "He said you were wasting your talents on that police force. He also said the chief was very condescending to you. We met the chief last night and he seemed like a nice man."

"He is. A lot has changed because of this case. The information Paul was able to get from the computer was invaluable, as well as his identification of one of the suspects, Reid Blake."

"We read about that," Anson commented. "I'm glad I didn't get any more involved with his mother than I did."

Rhonda's police instinct kicked in immediately. "You know his family?"

"You have the tense wrong, the word is 'knew'. I dated the mother for a couple of months, but she threw me over for someone with more money. She told me she was looking for a rich man, like Reid's father."

"Did she say much about his father? It could be important to the case."

"Let's see. She said she was very young when they met, but then so was he. He was married to his first wife and that he was thinking of getting a divorce. Something about her trying to pawn off another man's kid as his. He said he didn't mind paying for his mistakes, but he didn't like someone making a fool out of him. She asked him why he didn't publicly disown the kid. She said he was an important man and he didn't want a scandal to affect his son or his wife."

Rhonda's mind whirled. Was it possible Brad wasn't Karl's natural son? If that were the case, would he have known about it? The information certainly gave her something she needed to investigate.

"We've heard there have been four arrests," Paul's father said, when she was escorted to the family table for the luncheon following the funeral.

"Yes. The first two were Reid Blake and his wife, the second two were a lawyer from Madison named Michael Covington and his wife. The women have both admitted to being involved in the murder and have started divorce proceedings. Right after they committed the crime. That still leaves four co-conspirators unaccounted for. Two of them call themselves Sexy Diva and Reedman's son. It's hard telling who either of them could be. The other two seem to have disappeared off the face of the earth."

"I can't believe something like this could happen," Paul's mother commented. "Paul told us about the murder, then we heard about it on television. We also heard about the wife being murdered, and now Paul. It's just too much to comprehend. I don't know how anyone could be so cold-hearted to have committed three murders."

Rhonda held her tongue about the deaths of Sean and Donna Kelly. She didn't have enough facts surrounding their disappearance to make any comment outside the office.

Many other people commented on what a nice young man Reid Blake had been, leaving everyone in town not only shell shocked about Paul's death but also Reid's arrest. No one seemed to know the woman he'd married. That wasn't surprising, since after college Reid moved to Nebraska and lost touch with most of his high school friends.

By four, Rhonda was heading toward the lake house where she knew Kitty and Mark were waiting for her. She certainly had a lot more questions to ask of Kitty. With all she'd found out today, she was more confused than she'd been at the beginning of this investigation.

~ * ~

"We held dinner for you," Mark said, when she entered the house at just a little past seven. "I found some good steaks in Mom and Dad's freezer. I thought you and Kitty would like a break from eating grilled fish.

Although Rhonda knew both she and Kitty would welcome a steak dinner, she also knew Mark could eat grilled fish every day and never complain.

"How did it go at the funeral?" Kitty asked once they were seated on the patio for dinner.

"It was hard. Paul was a good man. Everyone in his hometown thought highly of him. I did find out why the carbon monoxide affected him so differently from how it did me. He had cancer as a kid and developed asthma when he was in his teens."

"That's tough. He must had had it under control to be on the police force," Mark commented.

"His family told me he did have it under control with the medication he took. Of course, it did weaken his lungs and made him react more severely."

"From the look on your face, honey, you learned something more in connection with your case. Can you share it?"

"Eventually, but I have to ask Kitty a couple of questions first."

"You know I'll tell you anything that will help find out who these murderers are."

"Well, then, I think we can talk about this without it going beyond the three of us, I met a man, actually he was Paul's uncle, who dated Reid Blake's mother. He said she was out for bigger fish. You know men with the same amount of money as Karl had. She also told him something else. She said that Karl was ready to divorce his first wife because he found out he wasn't the father of her son."

Kitty gasped audibly. "Are you saying Brad wasn't Karl's son?"

"That's what Blake's mother said. She also said Karl told her, he wouldn't disown his son and embarrass his wife any more than he already had with his affairs."

"That must be the reason Karl and Brad were always at odds. It was no coincidence that Brad went to Denver to run the office out there. Karl told me they had a big blow-up and Brad made the decision to leave. Karl wanted him to stay in the office here, but Brad wasn't having any of it."

"My other question is what are the stipulations of your trust fund?"

"If I were to die before Karl, the money would revert to Karl's accounts. The same would be true if I died before I could turn it in. Do you think someone knew about the stipulation and tried to kill me?"

Rhonda nodded. "Who other than you knew about it?"

"Just Karl, his lawyer and me. Oh yes, Susan and I talked about it. We thought it was a bit strange, but since Karl and I weren't planning to have any kids, it didn't matter. Besides, I was much younger than Karl. There was no way I was going to die before him."

"Did you know he had a bad heart?"

Tears sprung to Kitty's eyes. Slowly, she nodded her head. "Both Susan and I were concerned about it. Since Susan and I had our own sexual life together, we tried to talk him into slowing down, but he didn't want to hear anything like that. He told us if he died screwing, then he would die happy."

Rhonda knew this new information gave her plenty to think about.

"Have you heard anything more about Donna and Sean?" Kitty asked.

"I talked to Brad the other day. He said they were out

sailing and their boat capsized. The authorities said since the boat was in shark-infested waters it is possible their bodies would never be found."

"That's strange. I can't believe Donna is dead, especially in a boating accident. She wasn't fond of going boating with us, even out on the lake."

Rhonda's cell phone rang and she got up to go further out by the lake to answer it.

"Can you talk, Rhonda?" Jack greeted her.

"Yes, I'm alone. What's up?"

"We got back the preliminary DNA tests for the things form the mansion. It's a match for one of the DNA samples we found on Karl's penis. We also got another report about the other DNA samples. Susan was related to one of the women, but not either of the two women we have in custody. It looks like these two are a match for being related to Karl."

"There were only five people in on the Facebook chat, but that doesn't mean there couldn't be someone else involved. Can you get DNA for Covington and Blake."

"Since they're both charged with murder, it's already been sent to the lab, but we haven't gotten their results back yet. We put a rush on the women because of what we found on Karl's penis. What do you think we're looking for?"

"I don't know, but whatever it is I don't like it. I think we need to find Norman and Josie Ford before we can get the rest of the answers we need."

Jack said he'd keep her posted and ended the conversation.

Rhonda spent several minutes standing on the pier looking out over the lake. How could she tell Kitty she and her husband were sleeping with Karl's daughter? Since DNA didn't lie, it was evident Susan was Sexy Diva and had been the mastermind behind the entire thing. If Josie Ford was also a daughter, it was possible she'd signed in under the name of Reedman's Son. That being the case, Brad was in more danger than she originally thought.

Chapter Eighteen

"I can't continue to stay here," Kitty announced at breakfast the next morning.

"You can't go back to the mansion," Rhonda advised. "Where do you think you'll go?"

"I have a friend in Madison. I can trust her. She'll put me up for a few days. It's been almost two weeks and the two of you need to get your lives back to normal. I'll be fine and I'll keep in touch. No one is going to look for me in Madison. For all intents and purposes, I'm dead."

"Are you sure you can trust her?"

"Positive. I called her last night. We talked for a long time. She said she was so relieved to know I wasn't dead. We were lovers a few years ago and grew apart. Lately, we've been in touch. Maybe we aren't in a physical relationship any more but we have remained friends. As you know, that means a lot. If it hadn't been for your friendship, I don't know what I would have done."

"I don't like anyone knowing you're still alive. It's hard enough that a few of us know. The more people who are privy to that information, the more danger you could be in."

"Like I said, Rhonda, I trust Jacque completely. She said the two of us could take a vacation and get out of the state for a while. I'll be perfectly safe."

Rhonda couldn't help but think of what happened to Donna and Sean. They thought they would be perfectly safe on a vacation in paradise, but now they were missing and presumed dead. The same thing could happen to Kitty.

"Look, I'm responsible for you. I don't think I can let you do this."

"You're a gem, Rhonda, but I'm a big girl. I'm not a witness to anything and I know nothing about the conspiracy that killed Karl. I've also concluded I don't know anything about Susan either. I need to get away from all of this and being here means I'm not far enough away. I'll let you know where we go on our vacation, I promise. I'll even check in once a day, if that's what you want me to do."

Rhonda knew it wasn't easy for Kitty being confined to the lake house with two people she hardly knew. It would be much easier for her to be with a friend, but could she allow Kitty to be out of her custody? Rather than give in so easily, she decided to give Jack a call and get his take on the situation.

~ * ~

"I didn't like leaving Kitty in Madison," Rhonda said when she was sitting in Jack's office.

"She's not under arrest and since our co-conspirators think she's dead, she should be safe with her friend. I think you're just jumpy. Why don't we change the subject?"

"That sounds like you might have some information we can use."

"I do. Both Blake and Covington gave up their DNA and they're singing like canaries. It seems like they were able to give a complete description of Norman and Josie Ford. We brought in a sketch artist and we have a good composite picture. They also described Sexy Diva."

Rhonda held her breath. She wanted to see the pictures and yet she was afraid to see who they were. What if one of them turned out to be Kitty? She knew it wasn't possible, but the thought still niggled at the back of her mind.

The first picture she looked at reminded her of Susan Barclay but it wasn't her. The second picture looked nothing like either Covington or Blake, meaning Norman Ford wasn't related to them or to Karl. The last picture was one of Susan.

"Do you think it's possible Josie and Susan are half-sisters?" she asked.

"You know in this business, anything is possible. They could even be full sisters. It's not out of the question Karl had affairs with the same woman twice We need to look closer at the journals."

Ronda continued to stare at the pictures for several seconds before she remembered the CPU, they'd rescued from the rubble at the mansion. "Has anyone had time to work on the CPU?"

"As a matter of fact, the people from the county were able to get something they thought might be important from it. They faxed me the document and I made a copy for you."

Jack handed her several printed pieces of paper. On it were the names of the women Karl slept with over the years. Those who turned up pregnant had pages of their own, listing all the payments made by the company to them over the years. Each of the women were getting two thousand dollars a month until a child reached the age of eighteen. After that the children were given fifty thousand dollars for their college education. To Rhonda the amounts were mind boggling, but knowing the extent of Karl's wealth, she knew they didn't mean much to him at all. In other words, they were just checks that needed to be written on a monthly basis.

The names on the list of women he'd slept with was extremely long, but the list of women he got pregnant remained relatively short. She mentally counted the number of bastard children he'd fathered and realized there were only four of them, one short of the number of co-conspirators.

Hannah Blake and Regina Covington accounted for the guys, but the other two names seemed alien. The first was Joanna Thorson and the second Alison Nordstrom. It was possible Susan had changed her last name so she could make her way into Karl's life, but was her original last name Thorson or Nordstrom?

"These two names are promising," she said, pointing to the two women whose children weren't accounted for. "Do you think we have a chance of finding them?"

"That depends on how successful you are. You and Mark are good on the computer. Why don't you see what you can find?"

"I can give it a shot, but after this long, both Joanna and Alison could have married. Finding them by the maiden names could be difficult."

"Not if they were married at the time of the affair. I seem to remember a family by the name of Thorson living on Greenman Street for several years. I think his name was Arnold. They left town suddenly about thirty years ago. You could also check out Nicolas Nordstrom. He and his wife lived on Rogers Street about twenty-five years back."

Rhonda marveled at Jack's memory. He had a knack for remembering names of all the people in town as well as what street they lived on. Furiously she wrote down the information he'd given her. Since she was still officially on medical leave, she could hardly wait to get home and start working on her laptop to see what she could find regarding the two women.

Jack watched Rhonda leave the office. As much as he wanted her back on active duty, he knew she needed time to put all the events of the past few days into perspective.

It was a good thing the county loaned him the extra help he needed. Since this was a joint investigation, it was no time for his department to be running short-handed.

That morning he took a drive through the neighborhood where the Kelly house sat. With the crime tape taken down and the picture window replaced, no one would ever guess what horrific events took place there.

In Jack's mind, Brad Reedman was a fool to move into

his sister's house. Even without Susan completely off the radar, he had to be concerned about the Fords. As he thought about Brad, he wondered why he hurried back to the States so soon after Donna and Sean's disappearance. Had it been him, he would have stayed until he was certain everything had been done to find his sister's body.

~ * ~

Rhonda returned to the house, to find Mark glued to the computer monitor. "Come over and look at this, honey," he said as she dropped her purse on the couch.

She crossed the room and pulled the extra chair from her workstation close to her husband's chair. As she did, she saw the Facebook page for Reedman's Son.

"Doesn't it seem a bit strange that Reedman's Son is posting again.

She looked closer and read the post.

Hope you're lying low. Can't believe those bastard cops got Reid and Mike. It was foolish for them to take out that cop. I should have been the daughter. It was bad planning on their part. It's too bad it wasn't the lady cop. She's the one we should be worried about.

The words were so chilling, any response she could even think to make died in her throat.

"Do you think we should go back to the lake?" Mark asked.

Rhonda shook her head. "I won't run away from this. It wouldn't be fair to Paul. He gave his life for this case. I want to be the one to crack it."

"I know you do, but I still don't like you putting your life in danger over this. These people have proven repeatedly that they're ruthless. They've already killed one officer. They won't hesitate to do so again."

Rhonda knew Mark made sense, but she still hated

letting go. There would be no calming of Mark's fears, but at lease she could get his mind off the Facebook post.

"You know I went over to the office."

She waited for Mark to nod his head before continuing. "Jack gave me a couple more names to check out."

"Jack did?" he asked, his attention suddenly piqued and his tone sounding shocked.

"He got someone at the county to look at Karl's CPU. They sent Jack this information." She pulled her copy of the spreadsheets Karl kept on his conquests from her purse. "The last pages are the women he had bastard children with. He did recognize the last two as names of couples who moved out of town several years ago. It's not much, but it's a start."

Mark took the names and began his meticulous search through various websites. At least she'd successfully gotten his mind off the danger the two of them were in.

She was surprised when her cell phone started ringing, then remembered turning in the phone Jack gave her days earlier for the one she usually used.

"Pohs here," she answered.

"Rhonda, this is Donna."

The voice on the end of the line sounded like someone who was either trying to make a crank call or was scared out of their wits.

"D-Donna? Are you sure?"

As soon as she asked the question, she realized how stupid it sounded. The voice couldn't belong to anyone but Donna Kelly, even though she was supposedly dead.

"Did Brad tell you I'm dead?"

"You must know the answer to your question is yes. Where are you?"

"I'm at the Drake Hotel in Chicago. Until I can talk to you in person, I don't want anyone else to know I'm alive. Can you come down here and meet me?"

The request came as a surprise and Rhonda didn't know

what to say. Finally, she thought of a response. "I'm at home and my husband is with me. He's embroiled in this as deeply as I am. Can I bring him with me?"

"I-I guess it will be all right. I don't want anyone else to know where I am."

"We'll be there in a couple of hours."

She ended the call and turned to Mark. "We need to pack a bag. We're going to Chicago overnight. Can you see if you can make a reservation for us at the Drake?"

"The Drake? Are you sure we can afford it?"

"You bet we can. I just got off the phone from talking to Donna Reedman Kelly. She's staying there and wants us to meet her. If the city can't reimburse us, the county will. This is just the break we need in this case."

While Mark made the reservation, Rhonda went into the bedroom to pack a bag. She debated about calling Jack, but decided against it. If Donna wanted Rhonda to keep the fact she was alive a secret, far be it from her to break the confidence.

~ * ~

They hit Chicago just as rush hour started. Even though traffic southbound was heavy it wasn't the bumper to bumper parking lot she saw going north out of the city.

The closer they got to downtown Chicago, the more apprehensive Rhonda became over this meeting with Donna. Why would Brad have declared his sister dead when obviously she wasn't?

At the registration desk, the clerk handed her an envelope with her name on it. After taking the second electronic key for their room, she opened the envelope. Inside was a handwritten note from Donna giving her the number for the room where she was staying. While Mark took their bag up to their room on the seventh floor, Rhonda went to the fifth floor and the room where Donna waited for her.

Her knock wasn't immediately answered, but Rhonda assumed Donna was being careful as to whom she opened her door.

"Oh, Rhonda, I'm so grateful you're here," Donna said, just before giving Rhonda a hug.

When Donna finally composed herself, she closed the door and led Rhonda into the sitting area of the room.

Once they were seated on the couch, Rhonda studied Donna intently. Her appearance came as a shock. Her face was badly bruised and her left arm rested in a sling.

"Is Sean with you?" she finally asked.

Tears formed in Donna's eyes. "Sean is dead."

She began to sob.

"Can you tell me what happened?" Rhonda asked, when Donna finally got herself back under control.

Donna nodded and took a moment to compose herself. "Loretta and I went for a walk along the beach. When we got back, I decided to stay out on the patio to read. I'd just gotten into my book when Loretta came and told me Brad wanted me to come in the house. She looked upset, but I didn't want to ask what was bothering her. When I got there, I saw Sean lying on the floor, bleeding all over the place. Brad told me, I was the only one standing in his way of getting our father's fortune. That's when he pulled a gun and shot me. He must have thought I was dead, because when I came to, I was out in the countryside and Sean was beside me. I checked for a pulse, but there wasn't one."

Fresh tears fell from her eyes and silent sobs wracked her body.

"How did you get here?" Rhonda asked, when Donna stopped to regain her composure.

Her sobs were heart wrenching. Rhonda wanted to get this over with as quickly as possible, even though she knew it would be a long and complicated story.

"I was very weak, but I crawled out to the road and flagged down a passing car, I was lucky the driver was a doctor. He took me back to his clinic and insisted I rest while he called the authorities. I begged him not to call them. I was afraid if they went after Brad, he'd know I was alive. The local news declared us lost at sea and the next day we saw Brad leaving the island on a televised newscast.

Rhonda was stunned. "Brad arrived in town a couple of days ago. He told us you and Sean went sailing and were lost at sea. He's living at your house and planning to reconstruct the mansion. Why didn't you go to the authorities once he left Aruba?"

"I did go to them as soon as I knew Brad was back in the States. Like I said before, I was afraid to go while he was still close enough to finish what he started. Besides, I was too weak to do much more than sleep for the first couple of days. By the time I called them they'd already found Sean's body and were starting an investigation. They insisted I go back to the condo with them. What I saw there made me sick. There was so much blood in the living room I don't know how our friends will ever get it cleaned."

"Why didn't they contact us?"

"I asked them not to. I wanted to meet with you first. Brad is my brother. I thought we loved each other, but I was mistaken. Before any of this happened, we heard about Paul. I should have known from his reaction to the news he had something to do with it."

"Why? What did he say?"

"He said those dumb bastards think they've killed you. Thank goodness you were here with me. After he tried to kill me, I didn't want to put anyone else in town in danger. I said it was best if I talked to you before they did anything."

Rhonda closed her eyes for a moment. Suddenly, everything was falling in place. Reedman's Son was Brad. It was no wonder he hadn't shown his face at the murder scene.

As easily as the women involved described Norman and Josie Ford, as well as Susan Barclay, they could have implicated him.

"I do know what to do. Mark and I are staying here tonight. We'll go out to dinner and make our plans."

"Better yet," Donna interrupted, "I'll order room service. That way we can talk in private."

Rhonda agreed and left Donna's room. Before heading for the elevator, she waited until the security lock click into place.

Her key tripped the lock on the door of the room she and Mark were sharing. Once she opened the door Mark hurried to her side and pulled her into a tight embrace. "You look terrible. What's going on?"

Rhonda related everything Donna told her to Mark. "We're to go down to her room and order room service so we can decide what to do," she concluded.

Mark checked his watch. "It's almost six now. Why don't you change into something more comfortable than that suit?"

She looked past him to the king-sized bed with her new sweat suit carefully laid out. She'd packed it in anticipation of a relaxing evening. Now she would wear it to go down to dinner in Donna's room.

~ * ~

Jack finished his dinner, when his cell phone rang. Seeing Rhonda's number he quickly answered. It was entirely possible she'd found either the parents of Susan or the Fords.

"Are you sitting down?" Rhonda asked as soon as he answered.

From the tone of her voice, he knew there was more going on than the fact she had some information to impart. "I'm sitting down now, what's going on?"

"I'm in a hotel in Chicago with Donna Kelly."

"You're what? With who?"

"I'm at a hotel in Chicago with Donna Kelly," she repeated. "She's not dead, but Sean is. Brad killed Sean and tried to kill Donna."

Jack broke into a cold sweat. He'd waffled about suspecting Brad, but the recent happening in the case cast doubt on the man who stood to inherit the bulk of Karl's holdings. To have those suspicions confirmed, made his blood run cold.

"He's planned a memorial service for Donna, Sean, and Kitty for the day after tomorrow. He called me this afternoon and told me about the plans.

He waited for Rhonda's response. After everything that transpired in this case, he knew how her mind worked. It would take her a moment to formulate a plan of action.

"Where Brad is concerned," she finally said, "don't do anything until we get there. At this point we have the element of surprise on our side. For now, this is just something you and I know. Unlike the business with Kitty, I don't want the county to have access to this information. You know what they say about too many cooks."

Jack agreed. Ever since he'd received the call about Karl's body floating in Storrs lake, he knew this was his case. Cantwell's office was helpful in allowing them to use their resources and providing extra manpower, but this case definitely belonged to his jurisdiction. In his mind he could hear the annoying voice of reason. *You know it's not your case. This one belongs to Rhonda and with good reason. She's the one who has made all the breakthroughs. She deserves the credit.*

~ * ~

Rhonda ended her call and came back to the sitting area

where Donna and Mark were waiting for her. "Our timing couldn't be better," she said. "Brad is planning a memorial service for you, Sean, and Kitty for the day after tomorrow."

"That bastard. What right does he have to plan anything like that? He always hated Kitty and after what he did to Sean, to say nothing about me, he's turned into a real monster,"

"Calm down, Donna. This will work to our advantage. I plan to have both you and Kitty make an appearance at the service, just before we arrest Brad."

"Kitty's alive?"

Rhonda nodded. "Up until this morning, she's been staying with us at Mark's parents' cottage at the lake."

"So where is she now? Isn't she still in danger?"

"She is, but it was her decision to go to Madison to stay with a friend. I was against it, but she assured me she will be all right."

Mark remained silent during the exchange. He was obviously engrossed in what he was looking up on the laptop he brought down to Donna's room with them.

"I think I've found something," he declared, causing both women to turn to face him. "The two names Jack gave you hit pay dirt. I found phone numbers for both Mrs. Thorson and Mrs. Nordstrom."

Rhonda could hardly contain her excitement. "Since our dinner isn't here yet, why don't you give one of them a call?"

On a longshot, he called the number for the Nordstrom residence. He told the person who answered he was looking for old classmates and went to school with a girl named Josie Nordstrom.

Rhonda prayed he'd given them the correct first name. She held her breath until he finished the call. "What did they say?"

"I guessed right on the first name. Her mother told me her daughter married Norman Ford and they were living in Milwaukee. She even provided me with their address and phone number."

Rhonda took the paper with Mark's notes on it and felt as though she held the Hope Diamond in her hand. "I can't believe how lucky you got on that one."

"Since I did the dirty work on this one, you can call the next one."

Rhonda didn't like the idea, but she knew this was her job, not Mark's. Using Mark's phone, she dialed the number for the Thorson residence.

"Is this Mr. Thorson?" she asked when an older man answered the phone.

"Who wants to know?"

She hesitated for a moment. There had been stories about her all over the news. If this man was Susan Barclay's father, he might recognize her name. "My name is Deena. I went to school with Susan Thorson. I was trying to get a head start on the preparations for our class reunion."

"Don't know why you'd be looking for Suzie. She got knocked up in high school and didn't graduate."

"That doesn't matter to us. We're inviting everyone we went to school with. It should be a fun night."

"We usually don't hear much from her. To be truthful the only time she calls is when she's moving, so if we get any mail for her, we can send it on. My wife did have a call from her yesterday. She's moved again and wanted us to know she's relocated her practice to the Chicago area to be closer to her ex-husband and daughter."

The man proceeded to give Rhonda an address in Schaumberg.

"I can't believe it, we're two for two," she exclaimed, once she ended the call. "Once we get back to town, we can coordinate the arrests with the county and they can contact the authorities in Milwaukee and Schaumberg."

Chapter Nineteen

By noon the next day, Rhonda and Mark were on their way back home, bringing Donna with them. Rhonda prayed the plan they were able to work out would come off without a hitch.

Donna would spend the remainder of the day at Mark and Rhonda's house, with Mark once again acting as bodyguard. Once they finally returned home, Rhonda planned to go down to the station to meet with Jack, as well as Sheriff Cantwell. She'd told Jack she would call as soon as they got back to town, so he could have the sheriff at the office when she arrived.

When they pulled off the Interstate, Donna slumped down in the seat so no one would see they were carrying an extra passenger in the vehicle.

Even before the garage door could completely close, Rhonda's phone began to ring.

"How long before you get back to town?" Jack questioned as soon as she answered.

"We just pulled into the garage."

"Well, you can pull back out and get over to the Kelly house, on the double. I'm on my way there now. We got a report of shots fired."

"I'm on my way."

Rhonda quickly opened the passenger's door. "Donna, you go into the house," she instructed. "There's trouble over at your place. I need to get my badge and gun. I was instructed to get there on the double."

"You're not going alone," Mark insisted. "Donna will be perfectly safe here alone."

Donna looked terrified. "I don't want to stay here alone. Please let me go with you."

Against her better judgment, Rhonda decided not to argue with either her husband or Donna. Time was of the essence. She would insist they stay in the vehicle, well away from whatever was going on.

Emergency vehicles blocked the entrance to the subdivision where the Kelly house sat. Insisting Mark and Donna stay put, she pinned on her badge, pulled her service weapon from the holder, and got out of the car.

As Rhonda ran down the street toward the house, she passed two ambulances and a fire truck. In front of the house were several officers from both city and county departments.

"Who's shooting?" she asked.

"We don't know," Sheriff Cantwell replied, not giving Jack a chance to answer. "There was a call of shots fired about half an hour ago. We got here as soon as we could but whenever we try to approach the house we're shot at."

Without thinking of her safety, Rhonda knew what to do. "I know how to get into the house. Can I have two deputies?"

She was pleased when the deputies assigned to her were Steve Kline and Deputy Newman. "I need to go back to my car. Wait for me. I think we can get in through the lower level.

She remembered Donna saying she'd gone back to the condo to get her things. Hopefully, she'd picked up the keys to the house at the same time.

"What's going on?" Donna asked, as soon as Rhonda opened the vehicle's passenger door.

"There's been some shots fired within the house and someone has been firing at the officers. If you have your keys, I'll try to go in through the lower level."

"I don't like it," Mark protested.

"You don't have to like it. Besides, I have back-up. I'll be perfectly fine."

She wished she felt as confident about what she was about to do as she sounded.

Donna handed Rhonda the keys, being sure to point out the one for the lower level. With them in hand, she rushed back to where she'd left the deputies waiting.

"The sheriff says to give you this," Steve greeted her.

He held out a bulletproof vest.

Without making a comment, she slipped it on and secured the fasteners. She then led the two deputies through the back yards of the neighboring houses.

As quietly as possible, she slipped the key into the lock of the lower level door. She'd no more than stepped inside when she heard another gunshot and a man screaming in pain.

Throwing caution to the wind, she rushed up the stairs. From the kitchen, she could see two people lying on the living room floor.

"I shot him," Loretta sobbed.

Rhonda scanned the room. Loretta lay on the floor. Blood gushed from both a shoulder and head wound. Beside her was a handgun. A few feet from her, Brad was lying face down moaning in pain. Another gun was next to him.

Rhonda pointed her weapon. "Don't even think about grabbing one of those guns."

She kept her weapon trained between the two gunshot victims until the deputies picked up the weapons.

With the crime scene secured, Deputy Newman opened the door to give Jack and Sheriff Cantwell access to the premises.

From behind her, Rhonda could hear Steve reading Brad his rights. She wondered how much of what Steve said Brad understood. He had to be in excruciating pain from the wound in his back.

She turned her attention back to Loretta. Although she'd been wounded, Rhonda doubted either wound was life threatening. "Can you hear me, Loretta?" Rhonda questioned.

Loretta nodded.

"I have to arrest you," she continued. "You have the right to remain silent. Anything you say can and will be used against you in a court of law. If you cannot afford a lawyer, one will be appointed for you. Do you understand your rights?"

"Of course, I do. I've understood what this was all about ever since we were in Aruba. I know I don't have to say anything but I want to tell my story. I won't talk to anyone but you."

Rhonda looked up to see Jack looking over her shoulder. "Don't worry, Loretta, we'll make certain Rhonda gets to the hospital to talk to you. Now, you must let the EMT's take care of you."

Rhonda looked around the room. Donna's statement about how their friends would ever clean up the blood at their condo resounded in her mind. Considering the beige carpeting of the living room was now soaked in to only Loretta's but also Brad's blood, there would be no way anyone could ever get it out.

"Did you leave Donna at your place?" Jack asked.

"No, she and Mark insisted on coming with ne. They're parked safely out of the way."

"What were you thinking?"

"I was thinking about getting here. You did say on the double. Besides, have you ever had to argue with two people who are both stubborn as mules. Mark has some information we thought you might be interested in getting and Donna didn't want to stay alone."

Jack looked bewildered. "What kind of information?"

"By searching the Internet, he found addresses for Josie Ford's as well as Susan Barclay's parents. It took only two phone calls and we had addresses for both. Josie is in Milwaukee and Susan is in Schaumberg. I hoped they could be arrested during the time of the memorial service tomorrow and brought back here. With this shooting, I think they need to be picked up as soon as possible."

Jack followed her back to her vehicle. While Mark looked relieved to see her, Donna's expression was completely different. She had good cause to worry, considering her brother was involved in a standoff.

"What happened?" Donna implored.

"From what we can figure out, Brad shot Loretta, then decided not to allow the authorities access to the house. When she finally regained consciousness, she somehow found a gun and shot him."

"How is he?"

Rhonda debated about sugarcoating her perception of Brad's condition. "From what I could see, it was bad. Did you know he had guns with him?"

"I knew about the gun he took to Aruba in his checked luggage. It's the one he used on Sean and me. It's possible he found the gun Sean keeps in his office."

Rhonda looked at Donna, surprised to know there had been a gun in the house and neither she nor Paul found it.

"Since we don't have kids, we've never kept it under lock and key. Sean was a security freak and the gun gave him an added sense of protection. He also kept one in the bedroom. It's hard telling which one Brad found."

Rhonda was shocked to know there was another gun. If she'd known of their presence in the house, she would have looked for them while she stayed there.

"I need to go to the hospital with Jack. Loretta said she would give a statement, but only to me."

"I want to go, too," Donna declared. "If Brad is as badly hurt as you think, I need to see him one last time. He is my brother, after all. No matter what, we do have a bond."

Rhonda wondered how much of a bond there would be if Donna knew the truth about Brad not being her father's son, "I don't know…"

"If you think you're up to it, I think you should go to the hospital," Jack interrupted. "Seeing you could make all the difference in the world for Brad. Why don't you and Mark take Donna to the hospital? I need to talk with the authorities in Milwaukee and Schaumberg."

Jack's suggestion came as a complete surprise to Rhonda. This case certainly changed the attitude of her chauvinistic boss.

~ * ~

News trucks surrounded the hospital and reporters were everywhere trying to get an interview with anyone who might pass through the doors of the main entrance.

"Officer Pohs, can you make a statement about this morning's shooting?"

"I have no statement to make."

When they couldn't get anything from her, they turned their attention to Mark as he helped Donna hurry toward the entrance of the hospital.

"Do either of you have any comment?" one reporter asked.

Rhonda breathed a sigh of relief that Donna hadn't been recognized until another reporter approached her.

"Mrs. Kelly, we were told the shooting happened at your home. Can you give us any details?"

Donna shook her head no and hurried past the barrage of reporters with their microphones and cameras trained on her bruised face.

"At least they didn't ask me how I came back from the dead," Donna said, once they were safely in the elevator that would take them to the surgical waiting room.

The doors opened and Rhonda saw Steve and Deputy Newman waiting for them.

"Where's Sheriff Cantwell?" she asked.

"He's coordinating the arrests of the Fords and Susan Barclay with Chief Franks. They both insisted we come over here and be with you."

"Thank you for coming," Mark said, extending is hand to the deputies. "I'm Mark Pohs and I've been very concerned about my wife through all of this."

"We were told you can meet with Mrs. Reedman as soon as she's back in her room. The wound to her shoulder went completely through, so there was nothing to dig out. As for the wound on her head, the bullet only grazed her. It's possible Brad thought he killed her. There's no telling what was going through his mind at the time. He certainly wasn't rational. The enormity of what transpired over the past weeks finally took its toll and drove him over the edge."

"What about Brad?" Donna asked. "When can I see him?"

"He's in surgery," Steve replied. "They said it could take several hours, depending on the extent of the damage the bullet did. After he's in recovery for a while. It might be best if you went back to Rhonda's house so you can rest."

"I want to be here. I need information from Brad. I intend to get it one way or another."

An hour later, someone finally came to get Rhonda. She glanced over to see Donna peacefully sleeping in one of the recliners. Rhonda was glad to think earlier she'd covered Donna with a blanket the volunteer at the desk gave her.

"I'm coming with you," Steve declared. "It's usually better to have two sets of ears for something like this."

Rhonda agreed.

At this point she was so emotionally involved in this case; it was possible she would miss something important in Loretta's statement.

Stepping into the room, Rhonda approached Loretta's bed. With her left arm in a sling, her right hand cuffed to the bed rail and her forehead bandaged, she didn't look like a hardened killer.

"This is Steve Kline," Rhonda said, touching Loretta's hand. "He's a county deputy. If it's all right with you, he'll be recording your statement." She nodded toward the tape recorder Steve carried. "I also have to ask if you want a lawyer present."

"I don't have a lawyer. Brad does, but I don't want anything to do with someone who is representing him, I understand my rights and I waive them."

"If you're certain, we can proceed."

Rhonda turned at the sound of Jack's voice. She was surprised to see Sheriff Cantwell and the district attorney enter the room with Jack.

Loretta began to become agitated. "I don't want all of you here. Either I talk to Rhonda alone, or I don't say anything at all."

"Can I record what you have to say, so there are no misunderstandings?"

"You can do that, but only if no one else is in the room."

Rhonda turned toward the four men in the room. After Steve gave her the recorder, they left, closing the door behind them. Once they were alone, Rhonda switched on the recorder.

"Just for the record," she began, "I'm talking with Loretta Reedman in her hospital room at three minutes after five in the afternoon. Also, for the record, Loretta, are you currently waiving your right to counsel?"

"Yes, I am," Loretta said.

"In your own words, tell me what happened."

"On the last full day, we were in Aruba. Donna and I went for a walk on the beach. When we got back, she wanted to stay out on the patio, but I had to go to the bathroom, so I went into the house. As soon as I entered the kitchen, I smelled something strange. I found Brad in the living room standing over Sean with a gun in his hand. Sean was lying on the floor, bleeding. I asked Brad what happened and he said Sean was going to ruin everything and I had to get Donna to come in so he could take care of her as well. I told him no, but he pointed the gun at me and said, 'do as I say bitch or I'll kill you, too.'"

Loretta was crying so hard, she had to stop her narrative to compose herself. Rhonda turned off the recorder. It took all her restraint not to go to Loretta to comfort her. At this point, she couldn't become any more emotionally involved in this case than she already was.

"I'm all right now," Loretta finally said.

Rhonda started the recorder.

"When Donna went into the house, Brad shot her. I was hysterical. He slapped me and told me, I had to help him dispose of the bodies. We drove out into the countryside and threw them into some underbrush at the side of the road. We went back to the condo. He said we had to make it look like they were lost at sea. He let me take out the sailboat and he followed in the speedboat. He rammed the sailboat so it would capsize."

"Whose sailboat were you using?" Rhonda asked, when Loretta paused.

"It belonged to the people who own the condo. I wanted to go to the authorities, but he said he'd report them missing at sea. He also said if I knew what was good for me, I'd keep my mouth shut. After seeing what he did to Donna and Sean, I was terrified. I didn't want to die. I did what he said. As soon as he reported them missing, we left Aruba to come back here."

"What happened today? Why did he shoot you?"

"He started drinking as soon as we got up this morning. He was shouting about people I didn't know. I was so scared; I slipped the gun I saw earlier in the bedroom into the waistband of my pants.

"He kept saying, 'Reid and Mike were certifiable idiots. I'm certainly glad they can't identify me.' I asked him what he meant and he pulled the other gun he'd found in the house and shot me twice. I must have blacked out, because when I came to, he was firing through one of the small windows he'd broken out. He kept rambling about how the cops couldn't link him to anything. I still didn't know what he was talking about. I was afraid he would see I was alive and come back to finish what he started. That was when I remembered the gun in my waistband. I pulled it out and shot him before he could turn toward me. He wasn't my husband anymore. He was a rabid animal that had to be put down."

Rhonda turned off the recorder. Loretta did participate in the cover-up of Sean's murder and Donna's attempted murder. Of course, it was obvious, she didn't do it willingly. She did shoot her husband, but only in self-defense. There would be charges filed, but hopefully, the powers that be would take into consideration the conditions she'd been living under for the past few days.

"Did Brad ever tell you the reason he killed Sean?"

Loretta shook her head no. "I tried to ask him about it, but he said I knew too much already. He's mixed up in something, but I have no idea what it is."

Rhonda debated about telling her anything further but thought better of it. Eventually, she'd have to find out about Brad's involvement in his father's murder and maybe even the arson at the mansion, but now was not the time.

Loretta closed her eyes, making Rhonda aware of how tiring this had been for the woman lying in the bed. As quietly as possible, she left the room and went back to where the others waited for news of Brad's condition after surgery.

"Did you get anything we can use?" Jack asked when she entered the waiting room.

She noticed Sheriff Cantwell wasn't with Jack. "I have it all on tape. I hope they won't be too hard on her. She did what Brad asked, only because he threatened her life. I don't think she has a clue as to Brad's involvement in Karl's murder."

"I hope not," Donna said. "I've always liked Loretta. I hated thinking she was a willing participant."

Rhonda knew how Donna felt. She pitied any woman whose husband dominated her as completely as Brad did Loretta.

"We do have some news," Jack said. "The Schaumberg police department called and they have Susan in custody."

"What about the Fords?" Rhonda questioned.

"They weren't home, but the Milwaukee police are doing a stake-out at their house."

He no more than spoke the words than his cell phone range.

Rather than take the call with everyone present, he stepped out of the room. His leaving gave Rhonda a moment to relax.

~ * ~

"Franks here," Jack answered.

"This is Cantwell. The Milwaukee police arrested Norman Ford when he came home from work, but Josie wasn't with him. He didn't put up a fight, but insisted she should be in the house.

"When they went in, they found her on the floor. She attempted suicide. She's been admitted to St. Luke's. They're bringing Ford over to us tomorrow morning.

"As for Susan, she's fighting extradition. We'll work it out, but I thought you'd want to be kept in the loop."

"Thanks, I appreciate that."

"Did Pohs get a statement from Loretta Reedman?"

"Rhonda has it all on tape, but I haven't listened to it yet."

"Good, bring it over to my office and we can listen to it together. By the way, do you have an update on Brad Reedman's condition?"

"As far as Brad is concerned, we haven't heard

anything. It's possible he's still in surgery."

Jack broke the connection. Unless there were conspirators they didn't know about, all the players in the drama that unfolded over the past weeks were in custody.

He was just returning to the waiting room when he saw the doctor enter in front of him. Not wanting to miss anything the man had to say, Jack quickened his step.

~ * ~

Word of the shootings at the Kelly home seemed to spread like wildfire. Jack no more than left the waiting room when Rhonda's phone began to ring.

"Rhonda, this is Kitty," she was greeted as soon as she answered. "I just heard about the shooting at Donna and Sean's. What more can happen to this family?"

Rhonda quickly explained how Brad snapped and killed Sean, tried to kill Donna as well as Loretta. She also told her how Loretta shot him in self-defense. On the other end of the line, she could hear Kitty sobbing softly.

"I've talked to my friend and we're on our way down there. We're just getting off the Interstate. We should be at the hospital in less than twenty minutes."

Rhonda knew there was no use in arguing with Kitty. Over the past few days, they'd formed a kind of friendship they should have enjoyed in high school.

Not wanting to give away too much information to the people gathered in the room, Rhonda leaned over and whispered to Mark that Kitty was on her way.

"Do you think that's wise?" Mark whispered back.

"Probably not, but I can't stop her. She's almost here. She called me after they pulled off the Interstate."

The door to the waiting room opened and a doctor entered the room. "Are you all here for Mr. Reedman?"

Rhonda started to get to her feet just as Jack entered the

room behind the doctor. Deferring to her superior, she quietly sat back down.

"Yes, we are," Jack said. "Is there word on his condition?"

"Yes, it's good and bad. The good news is that the bullet didn't hit any vital organs. The bad is it severed his spinal cord. He'll spend the rest of his life confined to a wheelchair."

Donna cried openly. Even though he'd tried to take her life, the bond of brother and sister was still strong. What it would be once Donna realized they had no blood relationship was anyone's guess.

For Rhonda, the announcement came as a relief. So many lives had been lost due to the greed of Brad and his co-conspirators, she couldn't feel sympathy for any of them. She was grateful the nightmare finally ended. Had it not come to this violent conclusion, Rhonda was certain there would be more deaths. Brad stood to inherit a substantial fortune. His past actions indicated none of his co-conspirators would ever receive anything other than a bullet for their part in the events surrounding Karl's death and the happenings thereafter.

"Considering Reedman is paralyzed, this may sound crazy, but I want him handcuffed to his bed," Jack said. "He's my prisoner and due to the severity of the charges against him, I want every precaution taken."

The doctor agreed and left the room.

"Is that necessary?" Donna asked. "Where can he go? What harm can he do?"

Before either Jack or Rhonda could answer Donna's question, Kitty entered the room. Rhonda immediately noticed how the white capri pants, white blouse, and pastel tank top she wore accented the tan she'd gotten at the lake.

"Oh Donna," she declared as she rushed to the chair where her stepdaughter was sitting. "This has been such a nightmare."

Donna got to her feet and embraced Kitty. "I was so

relieved when Rhonda told me you were alive, I just can't believe Brad was behind all of this."

"Brad and all the others," Kitty commented. "I know they have at least two of the others in custody, but I worry about the rest of them. I, for one, know what they can do."

"They're all in custody, Mrs. Reedman," Jack assured her.

His statement caught Rhonda by surprise. She had no idea the last arrests had been made, Remembering the call Jack received just prior to the arrival of the doctor, she decided it must have been from Sheriff Cantwell with the information on the remainder of the co-conspirators.

Chapter Twenty

Two weeks later, Rhonda entered the courthouse for Brad's arraignment. While the others had been arraigned shortly after their arrests, Brad remained hospitalized and hadn't been released until that morning.

Joining Rhonda in the gallery were Kitty, Donna, and Loretta. After hearing Loretta's story, Donna posted her bail and along with Kitty rented a small house. The mansion would not be ready for them to move in for at least two months and none of them wanted to return to the house that had been the scene of such violence over the past weeks.

Rhonda took a moment to assess the women sitting beside her in the packed courtroom. Kitty tried to put on a brave front, but she suffered a double blow. Not only had she lost her husband, but also the woman she considered her best friend had been involved in both the planning and execution of the crime. In addition, an attempt had been made on her life, destroying her home in the process.

Donna lived through the nightmare of her father's murder only to have her brother murder her husband and attempt to do the same to her. As the conspiracy unraveled, she learned the man she always thought of as her brother was not blood relation to her, while four of the co-conspirators turned out to be her half siblings. It would be hard for her without Sean, but Donna was a strong woman. She planned to go ahead with the bed and breakfast she and Sean planned one day to open. The difference being that Loretta and Kitty would be her partners.

At Rhonda's insistence, Loretta obtained a lawyer. After many meetings with the authorities, he got the charges dropped both in the States and in Aruba. Although the physical wounds were healing the psychological ones would remain with her forever.

Across the room, Rhonda saw Jack enter the courtroom. Behind him, Sheriff Cantwell pushed Brad in a wheelchair. Dressed in an orange jumpsuit and shackled to the chair, he looked nothing like the worldly gentleman who came to the police department to report the deaths of his sister and her husband.

The judge entered the room and rapped his gavel for silence. "Bradly Eugene Reedman, you are charged with conspiracy to commit the murder of Karl Reedman and the attempted murder of Loretta Reedman. How do you plead?"

Brad's lawyer looked directly at the judge. "Not guilty, You Honor. We are requesting he be released on his own recognizance."

The district attorney glared at Brad's lawyer. "Due to the heinous nature of the charges, we ask Mr. Reedman be held without bail. The conspiracy to murder Karl Reedman ended in his murder and mutilation. After the murder of Mr. Reedman's father, his co-conspirators firebombed the home of Kitty Reedman to murder her as well. Following his father's funeral, Mr. Reedman went to Aruba where he murdered his brother-in-law, Sean Kelly, and attempted to take the life of his sister, Donna Kelly. Once he returned home, he tried to murder his wife, Loretta Reedman, and fired shots at the officers who had been summoned to the Kelly home where Mr. and Mrs. Reedman were staying. Under the circumstances, the state requests he be held without bail until the time of the trial."

There was silence, as though everyone in the courtroom was collectively holding their breath.

"The defendant, Bradly Eugene Reedman is to be held without bond," the judge declared. With that the gavel came down with a bang.

Although the decision had been made and the judge was ready to move on to the next case, Brad began to rant and rave.

"That bitch should be up here," he said pointing in Loretta's direction. "I wouldn't be in this chair if not for her. If my bitchy sister stayed dead, none of this would have happened. All three of those bitches should be dead."

His voice trailed off as an officer wheeled him from the room.

"He can't hurt you now," Rhonda soothed, patting Loretta's hand.

"Maybe I am safe, for now, but my testimony can put him away for the rest of his life. He planned Karl's murder on the Internet. What's to stop him from doing the same to me now?"

"He won't have access to a computer. We'll make sure of it. Once he goes on trial and is convicted you can put this behind you. Donna and Kitty have a lot to do to keep Karl's company running."

"We certainly do," Donna agreed. "We went over to headquarters yesterday and signed the papers for Kitty to take over Dad's position. That along with running the bed and breakfast, we'll all have our hands full.

"I've learned a lot about Kitty over the past two weeks, including the roll she played in the company. She's been helping Dad a lot. It wasn't a well-known fact, but he was in the early stages of Alzheimer's disease. He'd been training her to take over ever since the marriage, should the worst happen and he became incapacitated."

Rhonda smiled. *These women will be all right. They've all lived through their own personal hell and survived.*

"Rhonda," Jack's voice sounding from behind her caused her to turn to face him.

"I saw you come in earlier with the sheriff and Brad. I'm relieved things went well this morning."

"Did you ever have a worry that it wouldn't?"

Rhonda smiled. "Not really, but you never know what a judge will decide. He could have released him on his honor. I don't think that would have been such a bad thing, since he would have ended up in a nursing home. No one in his family wants anything to do with him. Of course, being on the outside, he would have had access to the Internet. This way, he won't have the ability to form another murder plot. In his warped mind, he thinks Donna, Loretta and Kitty should be dead."

"What I don't understand is the post he made saying there was only one to go. He couldn't have known about Paul's death. Wasn't he tipping his hand when he said one?"

"Not really. He heard about Paul. Loretta said he checked the local newspaper every day on the Internet. He wanted everyone in the loop to think he was talking about himself, when he meant the only one standing in his way of the entire inheritance was Loretta."

Jack nodded, accepting her idea of what was happening in Brad's warped mind.

From the corner of her eye, Rhonda saw Sheriff Cantwell making his way to where she and Jack stood.

"Very good work, Rhonda," Cantwell said, extending his hand. "Jack and I have been talking about your future in law enforcement."

The comment came as a shock to Rhonda. "I'm afraid this case has been a fluke. Out little town is normally quite quiet. Tomorrow, I'll be back on patrol and running the speed trap."

"I wouldn't be so certain about that," Jack said. "You know we've been running short-handed, but we're working on adding to our force. As much as I hate to lose you…"

"Just a minute, Jack," Rhonda interrupted. Are you going to fire me?"

"On the contrary," Sheriff Cantwell said. "I have an opening for a new detective and I'm ready to offer you the position. The work you've done on this case proves you have what it takes and you'll be a welcome addition to our staff. Would you be willing to join us?"

The offer left Rhonda speechless. Her mouth was open, but no sound came out.

"Close your mouth, Rhonda. You don't want to catch flies, do you?" Jack teased.

"No, of course, I don't. I'm honored. I'll have to talk to my husband, but my first thought is to say yes. We won't have to move and I will be doing more than running the speed trap."

Sheriff Cantwell shook her hand, then turned to leave. Jack also left her standing alone at the back of the courtroom.

"We didn't mean to eavesdrop, but we couldn't help hearing the offer Sheriff Cantwell just made you," Kitty said before drawing Rhonda into a tight embrace. "Even when we were in high school, I knew you were destined for great things. When I saw you at the door the morning after Karl was killed, I was shocked. I always envisioned you doing more than working on this jerkwater police force."

Rhonda agreed. When she attended the Police Academy, her goals were always high. Unfortunately, upon her graduation the only position available was in her hometown. It wasn't what she wanted, but at least she would be doing police work. Now her dreams were coming true, but at what price?

For her to move up in her chosen profession, three lives had been lost. Karl, Paul, and Sean all died, giving her a leg up in life. If it hadn't been for her investigation, she wouldn't have had the opportunity to use the skills she learned in school.

Starting today, her life would change drastically. It wouldn't take her long to clean out her locker at the city police department. She prayed she would fit in in the larger force and not be viewed as too much of an outsider.

Awake in a New World
The New World Book One

Caroline Lewis feels life isn't worth living when she loses her husband to Covid-19 while on a business trip to China. In order to avoid the coming pandemic, she opts to have her body frozen to be awakened in 2070. In 2120, archaeologists exploring the ruins of Los Angeles find Caroline's perfectly preserved body. As she is brought to life, fifty years later than expected, she is forced to learn to live in a world unlike the one she remembers from 2020. Aaron Phillips knows Caroline is special when he hires her as a research volunteer at the library. He hopes she feels the same way about him.

Unwanted in a New World
The New World Book Two

Orphaned at birth, Christopher is sent to a ranch for unwanted children. When he ages out, he is embraced by a militant group of skinheads who are unaware of his Native American heritage. A protest at an Alien Complex outside of Denver opens a new path for his life. While he is receiving his education, his new friends and mentors are working behind the scene to find his birth family.

Melian has come to the complex from the Alien base

under the Antarctic ice cap. She takes an immediate interest in Christopher, who now wants to be called Chris, and looks forward to see what their future holds.

Alone in a New World
The New World Book Three

As a child of four, Marco is all alone in the world. With only his mother in his life, her death prompts the authorities to send him to Henderson Ranch for boys. At the age of eighteen, he is sold into slavery to a ranch in Mexico. Two years later, he is recued and reunited with his childhood friend, Christopher. At his friend's insistence he modernizes his name to Mark and embarks on a journey that will bring him full circle back to Henderson Ranch, now called Resurrection Ranch. On his journey, Mark finds previously unknown family and love with one of the alien nurses, Kara, all of whom are willing to journey with him into the future at Resurrection Ranch.

Lost and Found in a New World
The New World Book Four

Peter was kidnapped by his father and sold to Henderson Ranch. There he worked without an education, until his eighteenth birthday when he was sold as a slave to a ranch in Mexico. Once he was rescued, he reunited with some of the others he'd known at Henderson Ranch as well as the mother he'd never forgotten. Helping his friends, Chris and Mark, he becomes involved in the rebuilding of the ranch where they grew up, renaming it Resurrection Ranch, where others like themselves, can work and be given the education they were deprived as children. Before leaving for the ranch, he meets Jerilyn, a therapist who will be transferring to Resurrection

Ranch. Almost instantly, he knows she is someone he wants in his life.

Reserruction in a New World
The New World Book Five

When Mark found not only his paternal grandmother but also his step-mother and half siblings, he is amazed when they decide to relocate to Resurrection Ranch to work with those dedicated to bringing their vision to fruition. Chris and Peter's families are also involved in the rebuilding what they hope could be one of the top ranches and educational facilities in the country. They are aided by several aliens who have come to add their expertise to the project. All is well until someone tries to sabotage everything they have dreamed of and built.

Redemption in a New World
The New World Book Six

When Mark found not only his paternal grandmother but also his step-mother and half siblings, he is amazed when they decide to relocate to Resurrection Ranch to work with those dedicated to bringing their vision to fruition. Chris and Peter's families are also involved in the rebuilding what they hope could be one of the top ranches and educational facilities in the country. They are aided by several aliens who have come to add their expertise to the project. All is well until someone tries to sabotage everything they have dreamed of and built.

The Return of the Ancients
The Aliens Book One

Nina is devastated when she realizes she must leave Plantas along with the man who is to become her mate, Ragnar, and her best friend, Tarena. When Nina arrives on Earth in Peru at the Nazca plains, she is greeted by a young archaeology student, Rand Jacobson. Even though she is attracted to Rand, she is still grieving the loss of Ragnar.

Ragnar is surprised when, after being greeted as a god on the planet Seros, the military opens fire on his family. After being taken prisoner, he is treated like a lab rat until a scientist, Geni, comes to his rescue. At her estate, he learns the physicians who work with her have saved the lives of his family and friends.

My Uncle the King
The Aliens Book Two

When three contingencies took off from their dying planet, Plantas, only two arrived at their destination unharmed. When the lost contingency is hit with a meteor storm, only one ship survives and makes it to their destination of Nalo. Over the generations, the descendants of the original refugees become the ruling class of their adopted planet. Even the rebel group, the Pure Of Nalo, are unable to unseat the monarchy. When relations with Earth are established, it is Prince Nicos who leaves Nalo to find love on an alien planet and bring back new ideas as well as his Earthly family to save the throne and the people of Nalo.

You Again

While attending college at the University of Wisconsin

in the 1960s, Carole Martinson fell in love and eloped with Phillip Vanderlin. When his parents realized she was a farmer's daughter and below them socially, they insisted they divorce.

Fast forward to 2019 and Carole is invited to a wedding cruise financed by her granddaughter's fiancé's grandfather. With no knowledge about the groom's family, Carole flies to Florida for the cruise she and her second husband never got to take. Upon her arrival, she immediately recognizes Phillip.

Phillip never forgot his first love. He is thrilled when he realizes the grandmother is the girl he was forced to leave behind so many years ago.

Sayo
The Secrets Book One

As an untried priest, Sayo learns he is to be like no other priest before him. His man god father, Zandar, he learns the new language of writing. He also learns he will find the joy of his heart and know of the love that surpasses any others.

Noya is but a child when her parents die and she is forced into a life of servitude as a slave to the high priestess, Dostra. At the urging of the man god, Zandar, she becomes part of miracle changing Sayo's body from boy to man. From that moment on, she relies on him to become her protector and teacher in the art of healing.

Round Tree
The Secrets Book Two

When Anthropology professor, Jocelyn Grant, Jaycee to her friends, meets her idol, Dr. Evan Clark, she knows she's going to support his archaeological dig both financially and by volunteering to work it for a summer. Even though she gets flack from the head of the university, her mind is made up.

Jaycee confuses Evan. She's a college professor, living in student housing, and yet she can make a large donation to his floundering archaeological dig. She also plans to spend the summer working with him. Something seems off to him.

When Jaycee arrives, Evan is immediately taken with her. When she starts hearing voices and having visions, he knows she can be important to him in more ways than one.

Umba
The Secrets Book Three

David Clark wants to put Round Tree and his family behind him to clear his mind. He's ready to return to the United States from Kenya to pursue a career in teaching when he receives a call from his family to authenticate a dig claiming to be a parallel to Round Tree. Like an old fire horse, he hurries to UMBA and realizes his true calling.

Leonore Hayes, Leo to her friends, came to work on UMBA in order to begin her studies at Havelan College with Dr. Jocelyn Grant-Clark. Upon her arrival she was told her job would be to clean the dorms, including the toilets. When she goes running, she falls through a sinkhole and discovers the archaeological find of the 21st century.

D.O.L.LS.
Desirable Older Ladies Love Specialists

When five high school friends form the D.O.L.L.S., they are each taking a month to find the perfect younger lover.

July – Grace is looking for a fire cracker for the Fourth Of July
August – Ellen finds a lumberjack, but it's hard telling

who will be climbing the poll

    September – Carol, the author, is wooed by a fan

    October – Marie, the dancer, kindles an old relationship

    November – Anita, the nurse, wants a someone to play doctor with

What will come of their month long flings, is anyone's guess.

Blood Relatives

When Lissa learns of her father's heart attack, she leaves her children with the neighbors and hurries to Chicago to be at his side. A military wife, she understands that with her husband deployed, she must handle the situation alone.

Paul, a Chicago detective, is set to testify in a drug trial and has gone to Wisconsin for his safety. Learning of his Uncle's heart attack, he takes the risk of returning to Chicago to be by his mother's side. Upon his arrival, he is reunited with his cousin Lissa. As close as brother and sister, he is anxious to see her.

About the Author

Sherry Derr-Wille began her writing career in her sophomore English class in high school. Challenged to get an A on the first test, she won the right to sit in the back of the room and write for a year. At the end of the year no one told her to stop the assignment, so she didn't. At her 40th class reunion, she realized she was the only one who enjoyed the assignment. It was too late because by that time she'd signed seventeen contracts for her work.

Wife to her high school sweetheart of over fifty years, she is the mother of three, grandmother of nine and great-grandmother of six. She is retired and lives in a mid-sized town close to the Illinois border in Southern Wisconsin. Her mantra is READ LOCAL AND BE TRANSPORTED TO ANOTHER WORLD.

VISIT OUR WEBSITE
FOR THE FULL INVENTORY
OF QUALITY BOOKS:

http://www.roguephoenixpress.com

Rogue Phoenix Press
Representing Excellence in Publishing

**Quality trade paperbacks and downloads
in multiple formats,
in genres ranging from historical to contemporary
romance, mystery and science fiction.
Visit the website then bookmark it.**